VIOLETS
—— *in the* ——
DUST

PEGGY LOCKWOOD

Violets in the Dust
Copyright © 2021 by Peggy Lockwood

Fiction/Mystery/Thriller

Library of Congress Control Number:		2021910509
ISBN-13:	Paperback:	978-1-64749-475-9
	ePub:	978-1-64749-476-6

All rights reserved. No part of this publication may be reproduced, distributed, or transmitted in any form or by any means, including photocopying, recording, or other electronic or mechanical methods, without the prior written permission of the publisher or author, except in the case of brief quotations embodied in critical reviews and certain other noncommercial uses permitted by copyright law.

Although every precaution has been taken to verify the accuracy of the information contained herein, the author and publisher assume no responsibility for any errors or omissions. No liability is assumed for damages that may result from the use of information contained within.

Printed in the United States of America

GoToPublish LLC
1-888-337-1724
www.gotopublish.com
info@gotopublish.com

CONTENTS

PROLOGUE v
CHAPTER 1 1
CHAPTER 2 3
CHAPTER 3 6
CHAPTER 4 8
CHAPTER 5 10
CHAPTER 6 12
CHAPTER 7 14
CHAPTER 8 16
CHAPTER 9 19
CHAPTER 10 21
CHAPTER 11 23
CHAPTER 12 25
CHAPTER 13 28
CHAPTER 14 30
CHAPTER 15 32
CHAPTER 16 34
CHAPTER 17 38
CHAPTER 18 42
CHAPTER 19 44
CHAPTER 20 46

CHAPTER 21 49
CHAPTER 22 52
CHAPTER 23 54
CHAPTER 24 56
CHAPTER 25 58
CHAPTER 26 60
CHAPTER 27 62
CHAPTER 28 64
CHAPTER 29 67
CHAPTER 30 70
CHAPTER 31 73
CHAPTER 32 77
CHAPTER 33 79
CHAPTER 34 81
CHAPTER 35 83
CHAPTER 36 87
CHAPTER 37 89
CHAPTER 38 90
CHAPTER 39 92
CHAPTER 40 94
CHAPTER 41 96
CHAPTER 42 98
CHAPTER 43 102
CHAPTER 44 104
CHAPTER 45 107
CHAPTER 46 109
CHAPTER 47 111
CHAPTER 48 115
CHAPTER 49 117
CHAPTER 50 119
CHAPTER 51 121
CHAPTER 52 124
CHAPTER 53 126
CHAPTER 54 128
EPILOGUE..131

— **PROLOGUE** —

For months now the small community by the sea had been plagued with stories of Witchcraft. The settlers spent most of their days fasting and praying for Satan to be taken from their village. Nora had stayed to her home not even stepping into her garden to pick vegetables that were rotting on the vines now as they grew.

She had seen many of her friends taken from their homes to be questioned and some had never returned. At night the sky was red from the bonfires set in the square to burn those found guilty that day. Husbands were turning against wives, brothers against sisters and even mothers against children. No one was safe. The village had taken the law into its own hands.

Nora hadn't lived in the village very long, but had established herself as a God fearing good woman. She taught at the grade school and was popular with all her students, especially the girls. She had become active in the local Church teaching Sunday School and organizing a Junior Choir. Why, just this week she had baked several cakes for the church supper because the girls had asked her to.

She was sure that no one would think of her as a witch but she was too frightened to leave the house to find out. Last week she saw her neighbour and friend Stella taken from her home next door and had not seen her since. She was so into her own thoughts that when the knock came at the door she jumped in fright.

She could hear what sounded like a group of people talking. She chose to ignore them hoping they might go away but the knocks became more persistent and the voices louder. One voice called out over the others. "Nora Preston, we know you are in there."

Why that was Jack Simmons, the butcher. Well for Jack she would open the door as his daughter was in her class at school and he and his wife had been her close friend from the time she had moved here. She reached up and slipping the latch on the door peeked out at the group on her front porch. Yes it was Jack and Bill Stewart the local barber along with other faces she recognized. "This is not a social call Nora," Jack said. "We have been sent here because you have been accused of consorting with the devil and practicing Witchcraft."

Nora backed away from the door in terror. They couldn't possibly mean this. Why would they think that she was a witch? "No," she cried. "I'm not a witch. You know me Jack as do you Bill. I teach your children. We sit together in church. I teach in the Sunday School. There is some mistake, you must know that."

"We thought we knew many of our neighbours," Jack said. "But as it turned out they too were witches. Several of the church women have complained of being bewitched and are suffering painful limbs and twitching in their bodies. There was no such malady before the church supper last week when they ate some of your cake. Everyone who ate your cake has fallen ill and it was decided that you should be put on trial for consorting with Satan. You will come with us now and tomorrow you will be tried."

Screaming her innocence Nora clung to the door. They would not take her from this house, for if they did she knew that she would never return. It took both Bill and Jack to free her and bodily carry her away. They knew that she would be a problem at the trial tomorrow and there was a chance she would be set free.

Since it was both of their wives who had accused Nora they couldn't take this chance. With a few short words to each other they decided to look after things themselves and carried her directly to the Town Square. There were others being hanged and burned tonight so what difference would one more make?

The fires were burning brightly as they entered the square and Nora's scream was just one more. Bill held Nora around the waist as Jack tied her arms above her head and secured her to one of the stakes. He tied both feet to the bottom of the pole and pulled it tight around her waist. Both men stood back and as they did they realized that the group that had gone with them to Nora's house was no longer there. They stood in front of Nora's weeping body alone.

One of the torch men approached them with a newly lit torch. "This one ready," he asked. Both Bill and Jack were silent as they knew that without a trial they could be burning and innocent woman. "Hey, is this one ready," the man said, waving his torch from side to side. Bill and Jack both looked up at Nora tied to the stake and paused for just a moment, then nodding they turned away.

The man with the torch moved to the stake and slowly began to set the hay on fire at Nora's feet. Suddenly Nora realized that she would not be going home tonight. With a final scream she called after Jack and Bill.

"You and all your descendants will pay for this Jack Simmons and Bill Stewart for you are burning an innocent woman." Both men stopped in their tracks but did not look back. Total silence fell over the square then there was only the sound of the fire as it sizzled itself into a black cloud and settled over all as the men moved away.

— CHAPTER 1 —

Rachel pulled her car over at the top of what seemed to be the main street. She had only the map, given to her by the realtor back home, to find her way into the small village. Many of her friends had thought her foolish for the life she was embarking upon and possibly they were right, but she knew this was the place she had to be and nothing could deter her from it.

It had been six months since she received the letter telling her that she had inherited property in a small village outside Boston. A distant cousin she had left her a house and the girls' lawyer was anxious to settle the estate and get rid of it. It was a family that Rachel had only heard of vaguely from time to time and then in whispers behind hands. So to inherit from one of them came as a shock.

She glanced around at what seemed to be a very pretty village. There was a centre square with one of those little bandstand affairs. She could never remember the proper name for them but all memories of the building brought back the sound of bands on a Sunday afternoon. She became aware of several pedestrians staring at her. Smiling lamely she gave a little wave and putting her car in gear continued up the street. The day had started out pleasant enough and luck on her side the sun had been with her for the entire trip. She had wondered at the azure tint in the sky and smell of salt air as she left the freeway and turned onto the single lane highway.

It was so beautiful and her spirits lifted for the first time in months. A bad relationship had been the deciding factor for this trip as the lawyer had suggested that she let a local property salesman look after everything for her and just take the money. Instead she did the only logical thing for her at the moment, walking away from her problem.

For some reason she knew that this had been the right decision and she was coming home. She booked a room at the local hotel, threw her bags into her battered up old Ford and drove away. Glancing quickly at the note in her lap she saw that her turn off was just up ahead. Slowing the car she turned off Main Street and the beginning of her life.

CHAPTER 2

The centre of town. Rachel had always wondered why all the small towns across the country started with a town square and most of the business areas were on Main Street. There was always a Gazebo. Yes, that was the name of the little bandstand in the centre square. There were also benches placed around to suggest a park area with some of the older men grouped around small tables smoking their pipes and generally just watching what was going on.

She was sure that at this moment she would be the topic of conversation. Turning the corner she saw along with the hotel, she was looking for, two shopkeepers busy sweeping the walk in front of their shops. It was a quiet street where not too many people would be enticed to shop but since one was a butcher and the other a barber she expected the locals kept them busy enough. As she slowed to turn into a spot in front of the hotel she noticed a small empty rather dingy shop two lots down from the barber. It looked like no one had operated it for many years and she felt sad that it had been neglected. She stopped her car and turning off the ignition stepped out into the street.

Neither men had paid much attention to the blue Ford with its' top loaded with suitcases and boxes until now. Now the sweeping stopped as both shopkeepers became aware of a young woman, hardly more than a girl stepping from the drivers' side and closing the door. She stood for a moment glancing up and down the street and then slowly moved to the empty store and wiping away the grime peered in the window. Brooms suddenly became leaning posts as the young woman reached into her bag and took out pad and pen to write down the number on the real estate ad. This they decided was not someone just passing through but someone to be reckoned with. Rachel was aware that she was attracting attention and wondered if she should speak or at least wave to her interested audience. Under the circumstances though they looked friendly enough she decided it might be better for one of them to make the first move.

Josh Stewart watched with interest as the young woman leaned into the window of the empty shop down the street from his barber shop. The shop had been empty for some years and most of the villagers passed it by without even a glance now. There had been a time when even the village children passed on the other side of the road rather than come near it. It had been passed down through generations like most of the local businesses in the village. Josh had inherited his own shop from his father as had his father before him. Nearly all the shops in Blakesville had belonged to old families. None of the children had even considered moving away after school as their parents had assumed they would take over when they retired and would keep everything in local hands. All of the shops were small. None of the large discount stores had been allowed to buy land. The local council too were from the old school and kept everything in the control of the village.

Josh glanced at his neighbour Jack Simmons who was also showing interest in the new face on the block. He and Jack had been friends since public school. They knew every good fishing hole and ball park in the area. Jack had always been the more aggressive of the two of them and was mainly responsible for their Friday night dates when they were younger. Jack still arranged dates for Josh even now that he and Sheila were married. Sheila always had a single girlfriend willing to double date with them.

He set his broom against the wall of his shop and made his way towards Jack. Time to find out if something was going on at the green shop. Just as he reached Jack the girl turned toward them and lifted a hand in greeting. When none was returned she got back in her car and drove slowly to the hotel up the street. Both men watched as she pulled into the parking area and made her way to the front door. Not just passing through Josh thought. With a knowing eye he turned to his friend and after a brief glance towards the hotel they both turned and went into their shops. It was time to bring the attention of the group who were in charge of the village business. It wouldn't do to allow the past to come forward again and bring terror back that once was the old way of the village. Jack took a large bandana from his back pocket and mopped his brow. Terror struck him as the smell of smoke once again filled the air and screams sounded in his ears.

— CHAPTER 3 —

It had been a quiet morning, a perfect day to work in the garden. Joe made his way around the house poking at each flower bed as he went. The summer had been unusually hot with little rain so he was putting in more hours than usual at the house. He did have other gardens to tend, but this was the major one as far as he and others were concerned. Even with the dry spell the roses and lilacs were as fresh and colourful as ever. Throwing his sack over his shoulder he made his way around the back of the house. He noticed spots that could use a paint touch up and made note to pick up paint the next time he was in town. Setting his sack and tools against the house he moved to the hedge that divided this house from the grey clapboard next door. Both houses had been standing side by side for many years. If he had to, Joe could probably remember the exact time that they began for he had been caretaker from the beginning and knew he would be for as long as he was needed. Suddenly he was aware of movement from the adjoining house. Just a slight flutter of lace curtains but enough that he knew he was being watched. This didn't bother Joe as he had watched and been watched for most of his adult life. The curtains parted slightly and Joe acknowledged a small waving hand with a nod of his head.

So Edna was in place as he was. Time for the cycle to start again. He stood for a moment rake in hand just looking around the garden. Most of it had been by his hand except for the roses and lilacs that seemed to have lives of their own. He couldn't remember ever having to tend the bushes and trees in his lifetime. All the bushes had to be pruned at least twice a year but the lilacs and roses all stayed trim and neat with no care. It had always been somewhat of a mystery to him.

There were times when his life here seemed like another time. Take the roses and the lilacs. How could they live with no watering or caring for? At times he worried about this. It seemed so unreal. Yet one look at the flowers and he immediately forgot how strange life was. They were like his children to be tended and protected as long as they lived. Yes that was what he was there for. To protect them for as long as he lived.

— CHAPTER 4 —

Bridgett stood at the window looking down over the garden. She had watched old Joe raking under the hedge. He had been there tending the garden since first thing this morning. It was one of her favourite times just looking out of the windows at her garden watching Joe tend the garden. The roses had always been the most beautiful in the area and numerous times she had heard

Joe boasting about them to different delivery men who came by. Even though Joe took credit for them she knew that the roses were solely hers and no one could take that away. The lilacs however were a mystery. She really couldn't put her finger on when they came but she felt there was someone else to claim them as theirs.

Dropping the curtain she turned into the room and once again felt the joy of the roses. Every wall was covered with pink roses. They carried onto the counterpane on her bed and the small chair in the seating area by the window. It was like they slipped under the window ledge and trailed up the walls. The filmy curtains moved in the window bringing with it a scent so familiar to her. Slowly she moved to the rose covered chair. She would sit for just a moment she thought as she settled back in comfort. It was as though the flowers were wrapping her in a soft pink blanket. The smell of roses grew stronger as she leaned back into them. Closing her eyes Bridgett gave in to the moment and drifted away on the scent.

— CHAPTER 5 —

Rachel stood looking out over the street below her. She could see the little shop peeking out between the two larger shops like a shy child nestled between two parents. She couldn't keep her thoughts off the little shop down the street. It was as if the tiny little building was beckoning to her and she was powerless to ignore it.

It had always been her dream to own a business but the opportunity had never come her way. Now in this small village miles from where she called home something finally seemed to be happening. From her window she could see the shop front and imagined what it might look like if she did in fact own it.

She was so deep in thought that at first she didn't hear the knock. Then her mind cleared and she realized that someone was at her door. Dropping the curtain she made her way across the room, but before she could release the door latch a note was slipped under her door. Bending down she picked up the note and opening the door looked up and down the hallway. The hall was empty, for whoever had left the note had disappeared from sight. Closing the door she crossed to the window.

She looked at the note in her hand. It had an official look about it. A no nonsense business paper in a typed envelope. No rose scented paper written by a delicate hand. But then who would be sending her a note like that anyway. More than likely from the local law firm handling her cousins' property and wanting to get the account off their books. Without further thought she tore open the envelope and opened the single sheet of paper inside.

Just as she thought it was a letter from the law firm of Johnson and Johnson that had contacted her about Karen's house. They had arranged to show her the house tomorrow and asked that she be at their office at 10:00 A.M. the following morning. The note sounded very formal with no excuse for her not being there as they directed. So much for having a short time to wander the village before attending to her reason for being here. Dropping the note on the table beside her, she once more lifted the curtains and glanced down at the street.

Yes, it was there alright, the slight pull she had felt before. It was like a magnet beckoning first, then holding her powerless and making it impossible for her to move from the spot. She could almost hear a voice calling her from somewhere. She leaned closer to the glass to see further up the street. The voice had a lulling sound and Rachel felt herself pressing hard against the window.

She let her eyes wander the short distance that covered the street until they stopped up short at the empty store. Then Rachel knew that the voice that called her was from the little shop. Slowly she lifted the phone and dialed the number for the real estate listed on the shop window.

— CHAPTER 6 —

Edna made a tch sound as she dropped the curtains and left her window. It seemed peaceful enough at the house next door but a watchful eye wouldn't hurt. It was an old house like hers. They had been standing side by side for many years each with its own secrets yet in some way sharing them. Edna felt a responsibility for that house as much as her own as no one had lived there for any length of time to give it any love.

Certainly Joe had kept the place in good order both the grounds and the house itself. Once a month he had a cleaning staff clean from top to bottom and he himself kept the grounds. Daily his truck pulled into the drive and he unloaded his tools and set to trimming and weeding. At times he had one of the local school boys helping him if the trimming became too difficult but she hadn't seen him for some time.

Deciding it was time for a cup of tea she picked up the tiny silver bell on the mantle and rang for Ella to bring her tea. Ella was the only servant she employed and it worked very well for her needs. She dressed like a floozy in Edna's opinion, flaunting around the male population. Bound to end up in some sort of trouble.

Hearing a car door slam Edna returned to the window and carefully lifted the curtain. She could see Joe just at the corner of the house with the local realtor making his way across the front lawn. The house couldn't be listed again she thought. Her hand trembled as she dropped the curtain and slipped into her chair. She was just about to lift the curtain once more when Ella arrived with the tea tray. Turning her back to the window she missed the curtain from the upstairs window next door as it too slipped back into place.

— CHAPTER 7 —

Dan walked down the staircase to his suite of law offices. It wasn't too busy today so he decided he might slip up to the little shop and take a peek. This had been pushed aside as something for the future as no one had operated the shop for many months now.

The old lady who had owned it had just disappeared from sight. Strange because when she operated the shop she was very evident in the village. But the minute she closed the door it was as if she just disappeared into the air. Not that she was missed but she and her young friend had been more than a little strange so the village was happy to see her go.

He realized that during his reverie he had crossed the street and stood at the side of his car. With a laugh he looked one way then the other. Then seeing he was quite alone he paused for just a moment to look around the village green.

It always seemed strange to him that although the park was kept well by the village caretakers there always seemed to be a burning smell. It wasn't noticeable during the day but at nightfall it was like many bonfires burning at once. You could almost feel the heat from the flames as you passed through the park. It was for this reason that most villagers stayed to their homes as soon as dusk set in.

Dan shook his head. Superstition he thought. It could rule your life if you let it. Turning the key in the lock he slipped behind the wheel and settled into his car. Just enough time for a trip past his house before heading home. Slowly he made his way through the gathering dusk.

— CHAPTER 8 —

Rachel pushed open the door to Johnson and Johnson Law Firm with some hesitation. From the time she was a child she had a bad feeling about lawyers. Probably from too many TV shows where they always seem to know everything and sent people to prison whether they were guilty or not. At least that was her fathers' opinion. How she missed him. He would know exactly what to do if he were here. He might also know why she had been left this house in the first place.

Closing the door softly behind her she glanced around a small but pleasant waiting room. It boasted one large window that gave more than ample light. Although furnished sparsely it was done in very good taste and did not belay a small village law firm.

The girl before her had her head bowed over an old fashioned typewriter busily erasing some small mistake she had made in the report she was typing. She was so busy with her work she was not aware of Rachel. Looking up the receptionist dropped her eraser and added a smile to her face. Rachel made her way towards the girl note in hand and smiling as pleasant as possible considering her fear.

Glancing over the girls' desktop past the typewriter to the old bits she saw more old bits and pieces of a time gone by. Obviously her employers were not aware or not interested in updating their practice for the girl was not privy to the day of computers and modern business practice. It wasn't any wonder she had put a smile on her face rather than a natural one.

Smiling as well Rachel, handed the girl the note she had received at the hotel and waited for acknowledgement. After turning it over in her hand once or twice and eyeing Rachel with some interest she offered a chair and disappeared through a door behind her desk. Well thought Rachel, settling down to wait, I guess I passed the first test.

Before she had time to get comfortable the girl returned with a dowdy looking older gentleman in a rumpled brown suit trailing behind her. He approached Rachel hand outstretched and smiling slightly. This obviously was one of the Mr. Johnsons' of Johnson and Johnson. After introductions he invited her into his office and closed the door behind them. Passed test two she thought as she seated herself in the soft chair before his desk. Now we begin.

It had taken the better part of an hour to go over the papers for Karen's house. Rachel was surprised to find that the house was free and clear of any loans or mortgages and was solely hers. She hadn't known her cousin but at Karen's age she wondered how she had managed to obtain such a property with no strings attached. She had thought the small savings she had managed over the years would have to be used to pay off a mortgage or at least some back taxes. But everything was up to date and ready for her to take possession.

This left the opening she had hoped for in purchasing the small shop she had seen yesterday. However, when she mentioned the shop a veil had fallen over the lawyers smiling eyes leaving her with a slight chill. Mr. Johnson rose from his chair and crossed to the window.

"A small shop," he said. "I wasn't aware of a shop for sale." Rachel eyed the man carefully. She wondered why the man who had been so pleasant and fatherly had become so cold and impersonal and why he did not know about a shop for sale. Strange as he was able to see the shop from his window. Even more strange, there was a note on the stores front window from his own office where she had found her original information. She felt a slight chill and wondered if possibly she was stepping into a dangerous area better left alone.

— CHAPTER 9 —

Jack Stewart set down his broom behind the front door of his shop. It had seemed like an ordinary day when he opened this morning. He was on his own today as his occasional help had called in this morning to say his wife was about to deliver their third child and he was taking her to the hospital in the nearby city of Boston. There had never been a hospital in Blakesville as bringing in a hospital also meant bringing in outsiders and there had never been any of those either.

For this reason a dark cloud had settled over the village with the arrival of the woman who was staying at the hotel down the street. It was evident she was not just passing through with all the baggage she had tied to the roof of her car. Also, her interest in the empty shop triggered something in the back of his mind. He thought about the shop and what it had meant to him and the other residents of Blakesville. He thought it was over but something in the air told him different. Pulling his apron from the back of the door he went back to the meat cooler to prepare for the day ahead. He heard Josh moving around next door in the barber shop and wondered about his thoughts.

He knew they would probably be the same as his, as most of their lives they had lived in each other's lives. Even their shops were side by side holding their friendships close over the years. Now with someone looking at their neighbours store they could feel something about to start. He had thought everything was over. All the smoke, all the screams even the crying. However, he feared he might be right and there would never be an end to their way of life. With a sigh he decided he needed a long talk with his friend.

— CHAPTER 10 —

Josh could hear movement from the back of the butcher shop. The walls seemed paper thin at this point because they were not part of the original building. Both Josh and Jack had realized as their business grew that they needed more space than the original buildings allowed and between the two of them they had added an addition across the back of the buildings.

The men of Blakesville had fought to keep box stores and anything not owned by the locals away and until now had been successful. The small shop up the street had been an exception and in the end had proved an error on their part. They had allowed an outsider to open a bookshop and soon found outsider was a word not to be used again.

Setting out the brushes he would need for the day he concentrated on dusting the chairs in anticipation of his first customer. He too was alone today as Bill his second hand, had asked for the time to settle some private matter at home. Since Bill was a good employee he had not hesitated in allowing him the time. Now he wished he had said no as he had a feeling that today was not going to be the good one he thought it was when he awoke this morning.

Settling back in the easy chair by the window he waited for his first customer. He didn't wait long for he noticed old Joe, the gardener, making his way toward the shop. As regular as clockwork Joe came every Friday for his Sunday trim. He glanced once more up the street towards the hotel where the woman had pulled in. A slight shiver went down his spine and he stood transfixed for a moment. Shaking himself, he gave a final glance up the street then he moved to the door to welcome his first customer of the day.

— CHAPTER 11 —

Everything in the village seemed to be upside down this morning. Dan had opened the office as usual, handed out the days' work to the staff and his secretary. It was a short day as the office was only open until noon on Wednesday giving the staff some time with their families. It was an old tradition carried on in spite of the rest of the world. It seemed it didn't matter about families anymore as most cities and even some of the less caring villages stayed open even on the Sabbath. Dan knew this would never happen here as family would always be first.

He walked over to the window to check on his car parked safely across the street. Everything fine here, not that there were hoodlums in the village but you never knew who might be passing through. It had all the appearance of a good day. The sun was shining and the village looked clean and tidy. He was proud of the fact that everyone cared enough to keep the outside world outside. Turning back to his desk he thought once again about his house.

Rumour had it that a new owner would be looking things over today to see the condition and name its fate. He felt weak at the thought that someone else might live there. Since childhood he had wanted this house. It had been handed down for years to one family who tied it up legally so no one could purchase it. Try as he might he had not been able to find a loophole that would allow him to buy it.

There had been hope with the last owner as he had become friendly enough to gain entrance into the house and was at least able to see the inside. Things were working to his advantage until one day Karen suddenly vanished and had not been heard from since. It was only after Dave Johnson had been notified of her recent death and had opened Karen's will that Dan found there was still another descendant to take over the property. She arrived yesterday and was staying at the local hotel. Dave had suggested she stay there as it was close to his office and easier to handle legalities from there. Also it gave the locals a chance to look her over before she took possession of the property.

Stepping back to the window he noticed that both Jack and Josh were in front of their shops. From the position of their shoulders he could see the conversation was not going well. It had to be the house again. Would there never be an end to this. Picking up his jacket from the back of the chair he made his way to the outer office. He would leave a bit early and poke around a bit. It couldn't hurt to have control of the situation should there be one before anything got out of hand. After giving final instructions to his secretary he made his way across the street to his car and drove the short distance to the house.

— CHAPTER 12 —

Rachel finished unpacking the one suitcase she had brought into the hotel. She didn't see the sense of bringing everything in as she was just registered for two nights. Plenty of time to move her worldly goods from the car when she knew where she would be living. She pulled a pair of rather worn jeans and a pink short sleeved sweater from the suitcase and laid them over the chair.

This would do fine for today she thought as goodness knows what condition the house might be in after being unattended for so long. She glanced at her travel clock on the dresser and was surprised at how late it was. Well no time for a shower now. She would have to be satisfied with a quick once over in order to meet Mr. Johnson downstairs.

They had made arrangements yesterday to meet at the hotel this morning with intent to visit the house. Nothing had been mentioned about coffee or possibly breakfast so she slipped one of the candy bars she kept on hand into her purse and finished dressing.

As luck would have it when Rachel arrived downstairs there was a note for her at the desk. It seemed Mr. Johnson would be half an hour late leaving her time for coffee and a danish. Seating herself in the small dining area she took a moment to look around. There were only three others at breakfast this morning, each at their own table and none of them seemingly aware of the others. Just people passing through she thought.

Rachel had always been a people watcher and would try to guess who the people were and why they were there. She decided that the man in the far corner with the old fashioned argyle wool vest and impeccable white hair was probably a retired lawyer or account executive making a trip to visit his daughter and grandchildren further south. His main interest at the moment was in his newspaper that he held straight in front of his face so she could not tell whether he was pleasant or just another grouchy old man.

Now that wasn't fair she thought judging him before she knew him. She could see her mother's finger wagging at her even now after all these years. She had spent so much time analysing the older gentlemen that the one woman was now paying for her meal at the desk and she wouldn't be able to get a good look at her.

At this moment the waitress set her coffee and pastry before her and Rachel decided to concentrate on her. She was very young to be working. No more than a school girl. She was very pretty and smiled as she set the coffee before Rachel. Rachel was about to engage her in conversation when Mr. Johnson came in.

Rachel waved him to her table and he crossed towards her. On his way he took a moment to speak to the only other man in the room. So much for people just passing through she thought. When he reached her table he extended his hand in greeting and ordered a small espresso from the waitress. With this he sat opposite her and settled for a few minutes of conversation. Now she thought is the time to approach him about the store he doesn't know anything about.

She had always imagined lawyers as old with grey hair, full mustache, at least 6'5", straight back and definitely a vest. What a surprise, she could see none of this was evident and she felt less sure of herself than usual. Bracing herself she set out for an eventful morning.

— CHAPTER 13 —

Edna sat back in her easy chair by the window. She smoothed the lace covers on the chair arms and thought back to when they had been placed there. It had been a different time, not better but certainly different. She could hear the sound of the clippers being used on the hedges next door by Joe. She smiled when she thought of Joe. They had spent many years together watching over the two houses.

She remembered when they had been given the responsibility and wondered more than once why they had been chosen. Looking around her, she realized that it had been many years since she had left this room. Nothing had changed. All of her father's personal possessions were still in place. His pipe on the mantle, his slippers by the fireplace, even the last book he had been reading at his death lay open on the table next to her. Nothing had changed.

She stood from her chair and lifted the curtains at the window. She could see Joe working away at the side of the house, red bandana tied around his neck a protection from the heat. She stood for some time studying the roses climbing up the side wall. Each day she studied the roses and each day she was sure that there were more than the day before. She knew that if she went to the other side of the house she would find that the lilacs had also multiplied during the night.

Grasping the window ledge for support she slowly lifted her eyes to the second story windows of the house next door. She felt a cold shiver run down her spine as her eyes drew closer to the two bedroom windows on this side of the house. Tightening her fingers on the window ledge she allowed herself to follow up the wall to the first window. Her body stiffened as she came face to face with one from the past. Tearing her eyes away she glanced at the second window where she saw a hand slowly raise in greeting. Edna dropped the curtain and fell back into her chair. She raised shaking hands to eyes trying to block out what she had just seen.

Had she really seen this person or was this just her imagination from the pressure of someone new coming to the house. She wished at times that the large house was the responsibility of another in the village. She longed for nothing more in her life than her cup of tea and one of her fathers' books. With a final peek around the curtain she sighed and settled back to wait for whatever happened next.

CHAPTER 14

It had been a quiet ride into the country. Rachel had hoped to pursue the matter of the empty store but Mr. Johnson had been very tight lipped during the whole trip. She decided she would find out all she needed for the house today and then with key and ownership in hand make either Mr. Johnson or someone else give her the information on the store. The more Mr. Johnson withheld from her the more she was determined to have it.

She had been so deep in thought that she didn't realize they had pulled off the main road. It was suddenly very dark and she wondered if the sun had just gone behind a cloud or if more rain was on its way. The road was lined on both sides with large poplar trees, one of her favourites. They were so close together that it was impossible to see light between them. Looking ahead she could see just a slight glimmer like the light at the end of the tunnel, or maybe in this case a rainbow. This of course was the reason for the sudden darkness, for as the car broke loose from the trees the sun was shining brightly once again.

Then she saw it, the house. Tall and stately it stood on a tiny knoll looking down on them. Mr. Johnson pulled into the circular drive at the foot of the knoll and turned off the engine. A sudden silence filled the air. Rachel sat with her hand on the door handle wondering if maybe her friends had been right and she should leave now before it was too late.

Mr. Johnson sat erect behind the wheel of his car looking straight ahead. He did not speak nor did he offer to open the door for her to step out. She glanced once more at the house. At one time she might have admired this house as it was magnificent and stood majestically in its' spot. Still there was something tragic about it. Something she couldn't put her finger on. The house itself shone bright and clean but she couldn't help but think there was something grey about it. She glanced over at Mr. Johnson who still had not moved nor uttered a word since he stopped the car. Yes there was something grey and she couldn't help but feel that he knew what it was. Still it was her house and she wasn't going to let some foolish feeling keep her from it. Grasping the handle she gave it a firm turn and stepped out of the car.

— CHAPTER 15 —

Joe heard the car coming up the long lane before it stopped at the front door. He knew the owner would be coming today to look over the house so he had arrived early enough to tidy anything that needed it in the yard. He was proud of his yard. His yard, that was the way he had always thought of it. Now the house was another thing. Not his and never would be.

The front door was as far as he had ever wanted to go. Karen, the last owner, had invited him in for a cold drink once but he hadn't gone. He wondered about her sometimes. They said the new owner was a cousin and planned on staying permanently. Well, he had heard that before. Not everyone took to the kind of life that the village offered.

Walking around the side of the house he saw her standing at the front stoop looking up at the front door. She was very tiny, not at all like Karen. He wondered if she would be able to live out here in the country with no one around. She had all the looks of a city girl and a pampered one at that. He suspected her long red hair was looked after by one of those fancy hair parlour places. Well best get over and introduce himself if she was going to be his new boss.

Joe chuckled at the thought of anyone telling him how to keep his garden. Standing his clippers up against the wall he wiped his hands on the sides of his overalls. Then glancing over his shoulder at the house next door he made his way towards the car. He had thought everything was over with Karen, but it seemed like the village was not over its life yet. There were still stories to tell and lives to live.

CHAPTER 16

Jessie closed the door behind her and leaned against the door jam. It took a moment to adjust her eyes to the dim light coming through the front window. She expected it would be much brighter when some of the grime was cleaned away. She could smell the stale smell from the shop being closed for so long with no one living here. The owner had been an outsider and when she passed away with no known relatives the shop had been taken over by the village for back taxes.

Jessie was also an outsider of sorts. Although she had lived in the village since birth she had never been accepted as one of them. Her father had died and her mother had left soon after leaving her as an infant with one of her neighbours to raise. The other children had shunned her and called her mother a witch leaving her on her own to grow into the quiet young woman she had become. Now she was on her own again left only with a small inheritance the kindly neighbours had left her at death.

Dropping her purse and jacket on a nearby counter she made her way through the store. She had always wanted a store and hoped that there was some way she could have this one. She had worked for Rebecca since grade school delivering the prize jars to the women of the village after store hours. Making her way to the rear of the store she opened the small door leading to the living quarters. It was like another world, Rebecca's world. Along one side wall were shelves ceiling to floor. The top shelves held bottles and jars of all sizes and colours. From the middle to the last shelf were books and magazines in great disorder as if just thrown there by someone either in a hurry or didn't care about them. The bottom shelf held baskets of dried herbs and flowers. Also on the bottom shelf tucked between the baskets were single sheets of paper with scrawled writing as if recipes of some kind.

Rebecca's recipes she called them. She had just started teaching Jessie some of them when she died. The rest of the room consisted of a long wooden table running down the centre and a small cot on the far wall next to a dresser for clothing. The far end wall housed a set of cupboards, stove and sink. Next to this was a curtained off area behind which was a small wash basin and toilet. Jessie sighed at how spartan the living quarters were, but thought at least they were adequate and would be her own. She walked over to the sink and turned on the tap, then reached up and pulled the light chain over the cupboards. Well, at least there was water and hydro. She was about to re-enter the shop when she heard a key turn in the front door. Slipping into the shadows she crouched behind the shelves hoping no one would find her.

Josh and Jack pushed their way through the small entrance of the empty shop. It had been some time since they had been here and both were a bit apprehensive on entering. The previous owner had given them a key in case something happened to her so they could get in. There had been no one to turn it over to when she died so it had hung on a peg in the back of Jack's shop until now.

There had never been a reason to use it until the young woman arrived in town. Dave Johnson knew about the key and called Jack asking him to go in and take a look around. Apparently the person at the hotel was the new owner of the Warren house and had also shown some interest in buying the shop as well. Dave would be showing her the shop this afternoon and wanted to be sure there was nothing there that she shouldn't see.

Looking around the main room Jack had a feeling of cold even though the day was quite warm. Probably just from the shop being closed up for so long with no fresh air getting in. He glanced over at Josh and noticed that he too was feeling uncomfortable. The word spooked entered his mind. With a nervous laugh he pushed further into the store. Nothing had changed. The shelves were still stocked with books for business. A long table down the centre of the shop was piled with magazines and picture books. On the back wall behind the desk that held the cash drawer and other business materials were the coloured bottles and jars of the old lady's trade.

She had made her own creams and lotions from herbs and crushed flower petals that she claimed would keep the ladies of the village looking younger and more attractive to their husbands. No one had believed this so she had sold very little in the village. Since nothing had been proved harmful they had left her alone to play at her little business. After she died they had simply locked the shop with everything in it and walked away. Now that someone was interested in seeing it, it might be prudent to have a look and make sure the creams and lotions were just that.

Closing the door behind them, they made their way towards the living quarters. Jack noted that everything was coated with a thick layer of dust. No one had been in the shop for five years since it had been closed. Yet as he neared the door to the back he was sure he could see faint footprints on the floor. Also the end of the work desk looked as if someone had brushed against it leaving it clean. He stopped and listened for some sound that might tell him someone else was there. There was no sound. Still something seemed wrong. He turned to Josh who was close behind him and noticed that he too was listening for something. For a moment longer they both stood waiting for something to tell them they were not alone but there was nothing. Brushing the thoughts away they opened the door to the living quarters.

Jessie breathed a sigh of relief. She had come so close to being discovered. No one knew she had a key to the shop because no one knew she had worked for the owner. She had delivered lotions and creams to the women of the village and surrounding areas. The women were afraid to come to the shop for fear the men of the village would think they were buying magic potions. For this reason Rebecca would take their orders, make them up and Jessie would deliver them when the men were not at home.

Rebecca had also taught her how to make some of the creams and lotions. She had hoped to run the shop one day and it might have happened if Rebecca had not died so suddenly. Now someone else was interested in buying the shop, leaving Jessie right back where she started. She slipped from behind the shelves and made her way to the front door. Opening the door as quietly as possible she left the shop and made her way up the street.

CHAPTER 17

Joe worked his way through the bushes to the driveway and the parked car ahead. He noticed Johnson was still seated in the car, while a young attractive girl stood looking up at the front of the house. No surprise. He had never thought of Johnson as being a very polite person and wondered why he had chosen the profession he was in where he had to be constantly in front of the public. Money he supposed that usually did it.

"Morning," he said, holding out his hand to the young woman. "I'm Joe, the gardener. I expect you must be the new owner."

Rachel turned to face a tiny little man in well-worn but clean overalls. He looked baked from the sun as if all his days were spent in the garden. She noted however, he was as clean as if he had just stepped from a tub of soapy water. Not a speck of dirt to be seen on his clothes or his hands. Glancing around at the well-manicured garden she wondered how he could keep things in such fine shape without getting dirty. Flowers bloomed everywhere and each flower bed boasted a well turned border.

Up one side of the house roses trailed as high as the roof in several shades of pink. It must have taken years to grow so many she thought. From the other side she could see just over the rooftop massive trees of lilacs. She was sure if she stepped around that side she would find that they too covered most of the building. The rest of the flower beds held a variety of colours she could not yet identify. She was sure she would spend many hours out here just enjoying the many colours and they were all hers. The slam of a car door brought her back to the reality at hand and she turned smiling at the old gardener beside her.

"It's a pleasure to meet you Joe," she said, reaching for his hand. "What a beautiful garden. Thank you for caring for everything for me. I don't think I have ever seen such beautiful roses. Do you care for them yourself?"

"Not the roses miss," he said. "Everything else in the garden yes, but the roses and lilacs look after themselves. They don't need my hand."

Just then Mr. Johnson stepped up between them and offered a key to Rachael. "I think it best that we get on with the business of the house," he said, steering her towards the front door leaving Joe standing at the car.

Had he turned he might have seen the slight smile on old Joe's face as he turned to follow the path up the right side of the house. Trying to fool her, Joe thought. Well it wouldn't take long before she learned about her new house and the secrets it held. It was alright old Joe would be there to watch over her. He glanced at the window in the house next door and saw that Edna was still there. He smiled; between the two of them she would be safe. He tipped his hand to the lacy curtains and continued to the back where he had left his tools.

It took a few minutes to fit the key in the lock. Rachael wasn't sure if the lock was sticking or if it was just her hands shaking from the excitement of everything. She wasn't expecting a miracle as the house had been closed for years now with no one tending it. She understood a cleaning crew came in regularly to keep the dust down but she never had much faith in cleaners who suggested they were a crew.

It had been her experience that these people spent most of their time visiting with each other and taking coffee and cigarette breaks. Single cleaners were far more efficient as they usually counted on their reputation for the next job. Not some big office that doled out cleaners like bags of popcorn. So when she entered the front hall her thought was surprise.

It was clean. Everything polished and not a speck of dust in sight. Her second thought was that a window must be broken and the roses from the side wall had grown into the house as the fragrance of roses filled the air. On further inspection she realized that the roses were in the wallpaper. Hundreds of roses wound their way up the staircase and out of sight.

She stepped up to the first landing for further inspection and found to her surprise that tiny lilacs were intertwined among the roses and that they too were making their way up the stairs. It was as though they each found solace with each other bringing a kind of peace to both.

Rachel felt a slight shiver as if a cold breeze had found its way into the house. Backing down the stairs she glanced over at Mr. Johnson to see if he too had felt the cold but once again he stood as if a statue staring straight ahead. Suddenly the air became warm again and the fragrance was gone.

Rachel turned to move further into the house. How foolish she thought. Just nerves with a new house and possibly a business in town. Things could not be better. Putting a smile on her face she continued down the hall to the next room. There was so much to see and she didn't want to waste any time with her own foolishness. She opened the door straight ahead of her and found herself in a small but charming kitchen. Everything seemed warm and bright and she soon forgot the coldness of the front hall.

— CHAPTER 18 —

Dan drove slowly up the road for home, thoughts running through his head. The village had been quiet for some time now and he reconciled himself with the fact he would not be getting the house yet. For a while when Karen lived there it looked like he was finally going to fulfill his dream.

It had been a surprise the day he arrived and found the broken door and no one around. He had called out but the house had been empty. It had been too late that night to do any repairs so he had left to return the next morning with new wood and tools to repair the damage. Once again this morning he called out but everything had been still and quiet. When the repairs were finished he went through the house to see if there was any further damage. But found nothing out of place.

On inspecting the upstairs he found the bedrooms and bathroom also tidy and clean as if the cleaners had just finished their monthly visit. It was a puzzle for he and Karen had been slowly building a relationship that looked to be more than just the friendship formed on their first meeting.

Making his way down the stairs he glanced at the wall to his left. The wallpaper here had always been a fascination for him. Once he thought there had just been roses winding their way from floor to ceiling. Looking now he could see bunches of purple lilacs interspersed through the vines. Odd he hadn't noticed them before. Leaning forward for a better look he felt a slight pull and the scent of the flowers became overpowering. He felt himself falling into darkness and reaching back took hold of the banister to keep from falling down the stairs. For some minutes he stood like this until once again his head began to clear and the fragrance disappeared. He looked at the wallpaper in front of him and realized that is was just roses. The lilacs were gone.

Moving slowly down the stairs he made his way to the front door. Anything else that had to be done could be done another day he thought. Checking the lock on the new door he glanced once more at the wallpaper in the staircase. The sun from the open door shone on the pink roses trailing up the wall and once again interspersed through the pink was the deep colour of purple lilacs.

He felt as if the whole experience was just a thought in his mind. A cold shiver coursed through his body and he began to lose consciousness. He knew he had to get away. Moving to the door Dan stepped out onto the front porch and locked the door behind him.

— CHAPTER 19 —

Sheriff Hennessey leaned back in his chair, coffee in hand. He glanced out the window at what looked like the start of a beautiful day. The sun was shining and already some of the villagers were making their way down the street toward the shops. Most of the shops were opened early as the owners were not lay a beds like some in the larger cities close by. It had always been their practice to be up and at it as soon as the sun came up ready to serve their customers.

If he moved his chair forward he would be able to see Jack Simmons and Josh Stewart slipping their keys into the doors of their respective shops at this moment. Both Jack and Josh had carried on the family business after their fathers had passed on and most people could be heard to say it was as if no hands had changed at all. Both men had attended school together and had been fast friends since. Most Sundays they could be found at the small pond at the end of the village quietly sitting with their fishing poles bobbing in the current. Not that they ever caught much but the companionship seemed to be all that they needed.

As a few more of the villagers made their way up the street the sheriff turned his chair back to his desk and prepared for another work day. Sorting through the papers on his desk he found a note from Jack Simmons. It must have been put there the preceding day by his assistant Fred. He noted the urgent at the top of the page and smiled. All of Fred's notes were labelled urgent.

He remembered when the Jones' cat climbed the tree out front of their house and wouldn't come down there had been an urgent note in capital letters from Fred for a rescue team. By the time the team had arrived at the Jones' place the cat was curled up in the chair on the front porch watching with interest all the fuss around it. With just a glance he pushed the note on the pick on his desk to be tended to later and pushed back his chair. It was time to make his way down to the coffee shop for the first news of the day.

— CHAPTER 20 —

Rachel stood at the bedroom window looking out over the garden. She had assured Mr. Johnson that she would be fine left alone in the house and after a short argument saw him out the door. Making her way down the stairs to the kitchen she found a few provisions had been laid in for her so there was nothing to take her back to the village at the moment.

Mr. Johnson said he would have her car brought out to her in the morning, so she had only to wait for it to further shop for things she would need. On checking the cupboards she found the provisions were few as if whoever put them in did not think that she would be staying. Finding coffee, tea and sugar she decided that this would be enough for the moment and after putting the kettle on to boil she set about checking the rest of the house.

Off the hall was a pleasant looking, what might be called a sitting room. The furniture was very old but in prime condition so nothing had to be replaced here. A group of pictures stood on the mantle of an old but clean fireplace which she noticed had been newly set with logs. This would be a wonderful place to sit reading in the evening. She made her way through the room touching small trinkets here and there until once again she was at the doorway.

Looking across the hall she found a formal dining room with equally old furnishings. However, this room was not as inviting as the sitting room and she hesitated entering for now. Suddenly aware that the kettle was boiling she made her way once more into the kitchen. Pouring water over a tea bag in her cup she began her tour of the kitchen.

As with the other rooms everything was spotless. The gardener, who was in charge of the house since Karen left, certainly made sure the cleaning staff earned their money. She must be sure to thank him at the first opportunity. This room seemed the brightest of all. The window over the kitchen sink sparkled from clean cloths and elbow grease. Now that was an old saying Rachel thought. I wonder where I heard that. Not from her folks as they had been right up on all the modern ways and made sure she was too.

She stepped over to the window and lifted the curtains to see out into the yard. From here she could see far into the adjoining fields. It was as if the hills rolled right down into her yard and ended at the house. She didn't think that there were hills, but as she stood there she had the sensation of lights coming over hills. Also the fragrance of the lilacs on this side of the house seemed to overpower her as she stood there.

Dropping the curtains she stepped back into the room and the fragrance dissipated. For a moment she stood still looking around her. Where was she? Then just as suddenly she was back in the kitchen holding her cup of tea. Day dreaming she thought setting her cup on the table. Just too much excitement with the house and business all in one day. She shook herself and said "pull yourself together Rachel and see what you have inherited." With a little laugh she turned towards the kitchen door. Leaving her tea she started back up the hall to the staircase and the second floor. Time to look over the rest of the house.

CHAPTER 21

Dan pulled into his driveway to find two cars waiting for him. He wasn't expecting company and quite on the contrary was a bit upset at having some. On further inspection he realized it to be Josh and Jack leaning against their vehicles smoking in the dusk. This could only mean trouble as neither of the men spent much time in anyone else's company but their own. They were, however, both members of the village council and did take this part of their lives very seriously. Well, best face it and get it over with he thought.

Putting his car in park he stepped out onto the drive in front of the two men. Josh and Jack had been waiting for some time. It was past the time that Dan should have arrived home, but they decided he must have driven past that tiresome house again. The house had been a problem for many years for the village but there had been nothing they could do about it. It had been protected against being sold or torn down unless by a descendent of the original family.

They had thought when the last girl had disappeared that the problem had finally come to an end. However, Dave

Johnson had informed them that a distant cousin had inherited the house and would be coming to look the place over. Now she was here and staying at the local hotel. A further conversation with Dave also told them that she was planning to stay and was also interested in Rebecca's old store on the main street.

Jack shook his head and stamped out his cigarette in the dust. They needed to talk to Dan to see where they should go from here, thus the visit tonight. Both men stepped forward, hands extended as Dan approached.

"To what pleasure gentlemen," Dan asked? Jack took another step forward saying, "I suppose you drove by the house on your way home. Still hoping to buy it?" "That's the plan," Dan replied. "Someday Dave Johnson will find a loophole in the paperwork and the house will be mine. Then the village problems will be over and we can go on with living." "What was the reason you felt it necessary to drive out here at this time of the day?" Dan asked.

Jack waited a moment before speaking. "Dan you know the history of that house and you know how Josh and I are involved. This is nothing of our doing. We are bound to it by the actions of our families. As long as that house stands we are tied to it and what it becomes. You have to come up with something to release us and yourself. You have to find a way to buy that house and release the village."

Dan eyed both men standing before him. He knew they were right and asked them to follow him to the Warren house. When Karen had the house he almost had it, but now here he was again looking to another way. He couldn't be sure that this girl would be as easy to manipulate as Karen. With a final word to the two men he made his way to the front door and let himself and them in. Tomorrow looked like it was going to be a long one.

The air was very stale and it felt as if the house had been closed up for many years rather than just months. A stream of light worked its way through the front door and across the hall. The air began to clear and hundreds of tiny rosebuds seem to burst into bloom as the door worked its way open further.

The three men stood in silence as the walls seemed to move as they did into the room. It was as if the garden had pulled up all of its soil and moved inside. There was no sound. Only a heaviness laying over them and a silence pushing down out of the fragrance of roses from the walls. All was still.

Suddenly the silence broke and sunlight spread through the doorway. Once again it was just a sun filled hallway with three men standing courageously in the hall.

CHAPTER 22

Josh pulled his car out of Dan's laneway. He wondered why any of this should affect him as none of it had been his problem. The only problem he had was being born a Stewart and carrying on the family name. Not only the Stewart name but also the name Josh. Relatives over the years had spoken of another Josh but none had ever revealed to him what the man had done.

There were many secrets in the village with no one wanting to speak of them. Mostly it was whispers and never when he was close enough to hear. Jack had complained about the same thing. As boys they had tried to catch adult conversations by hiding behind doors or listening through air vents. They had never been able to catch more than a few words at a time and couldn't fit them into any kind of sense.

As they grew older the novelty wore off and they just let it go. There were so many things in the village that puzzled him. Jack would just shrug it off as not important, but not Josh. One thing he couldn't understand was why the old house on the hill was protected and why at nightfall the centre square always had the smell of smoke. He decided it was time he found out. He waved at Jack as he passed to go on to his own house sitting back with knowledge that he was finally going to do something about his heritage.

— CHAPTER 23 —

Rachel awoke to a fresh breeze ruffling her bedroom curtains. She rolled over and pulled the soft counterpane up around her chin. She had never felt such peace as she had since coming to this house. She peeked over the fluffy bed covers at the frothy curtains moving in the breeze.

Soft sunlight picked its way across the room and fell on the bed beside her. She could just lie here all day and enjoy she thought as she snuggled further into the massive bed. Her life seemed less complicated since she arrived in the village and she quietly thanked her cousin Karen for making her life liveable.

A sudden noise from the garden brought her from her reverie and she threw the covers back and stepped into her slippers. Pulling the curtains aside she realized it was Joe the gardener going about his morning chores. She wondered if he intended to stay on for her and just what the charge might be. Well, now might just be the time to talk to him about what arrangements they might come to. It certainly would be good to have him as this garden looked like it would be a great deal of work. Hastily she slipped into what she called her work clothes and pulling a brush through her hair she hurried down the hall and out the front door.

CHAPTER 24

Jessie peeked through the dust on the front window of the shop. She had been staying in the living quarters at the back of the shop for several weeks now. Watching closely she had managed to stay clear of anyone coming in the shop so had remained undetected. By rights she shouldn't have to hide the fact that she was living there for Rebecca had always intended for her to have the shop when she passed on. However, Rebecca had passed so suddenly there had been no time to make things legal so the store had been closed.

Jessie had no claim on the store except verbally from Rebecca so she found herself out on the street. She had a bit of savings from what Rebecca had given her but nothing near the amount it would take to buy the store. Rebecca had taught her well and she knew that she could make the potions and creams that Rebecca sold to the ladies of the village herself. It would not pay to make this known however, as the ladies bought these products without the knowledge of their husbands. Rebecca had sold them in secret from her back room using the front of her store to sell books.

The village at one time had been known for practising witchcraft so it would not do well for the men to think that the practice was back. She stepped back into the room and looked over what had one time been stacked with books and small ornaments. It was mostly dust now as nothing had been cared for since Rebecca's death. Jessie fingered some of the small items on the table near her. How sad all these lovely things were just sitting waiting for a home never to leave this dusty place. Sighing she made her way to the living quarters at the back that she now called home to make her morning tea.

CHAPTER 25

Rachel wanted the store. She had been living in the village for over a week and was settled comfortably into her house. Everything had been kept so well she had very little to do except unpack her boxes and refurbish the food supplies. She had marvelled at how for a small village everything could be had. The grocery store stocked everything one could possibly need. There was a well-stocked hardware store, a pharmacy and a very up to date clothing store. With all the usual small shops a library and quaint little restaurants she couldn't see that there would be any need for her to leave the village again.

For just an instant she wondered why Karen had felt the need to leave so mysteriously but quickly put that from her mind as she thought had it not been for this her good fortune would not have happened. She had missed her talk with the gardener as by the time she had dressed he was pulling up the lane and away from the house. She decided she would have to be up earlier if she wanted to catch him.

Settling in her chair at the kitchen table sipping her tea she began to make a list of things to be done for the day. First and foremost was a call to Mr. Johnson about the purchase of the store. She had called every day for the past week and he still had not returned her call. His secretary said he was out of the office but she would have him call when he returned. Now after a week she decided if he didn't answer this morning she was going to his office and sit there until he returned from whatever important thing had kept him so busy he couldn't at least pick up a phone.

She felt a slight prickle of annoyance that could very easily turn into anger if not controlled. She had no idea why the sale of a small bookshop would be such a problem that he had to dance around contacting her. Shaking herself she pushed back her chair and made her way to the sink with her tea cup. Glancing out the kitchen window she decided she wasn't going to ruin such a beautiful day by starting off angry. She would just check over a few things and head into the village to the lawyer's office and buy a store.

That she decided was her final word, and then checking to make sure everything was turned off and safe for the day she headed for the front door and freedom for the balance of the day. She smiled to hear the click of the front door as it closed behind her.

CHAPTER 26

Dave Johnson arrived at the office early this morning. His secretary would not be in for another hour so he made and poured himself a coffee and settled behind his desk. He knew today he would have to face the new owner of the Warren house and he did not relish the idea. There was nothing he could do about the small book store up the street from his office. He had searched every possibility and found no reason to refuse Rachel. He had Joyce draw up the papers the day before and now had only to call Rachel and have her come to the office. He could see this as a problem in the future and wished he had never seen the Warren house. The village was a quiet place and very seldom did a problem come across his desk. Everyone lived a quiet life with no crime to speak of so his life was made up of new mortgages on houses for existing tenants and wills for the old folks. Now that there was a new owner at the Warren house he knew his life would change again. He had called a meeting with the other business owners, at least with the ones that had to make a decision about the book shop. He had searched every way possible not to sell it but after searching every possibility he knew they had no choice but to let this girl have the store.

During the search he had found that there had been just one concession in Rebecca's will and that had been that with the sale the shop girl Jessie would be kept on by the new owner for a period of one year. Also, she would be able to live in the quarters at the back of the shop.

He knew for a fact that Jessie had been living there for some time. She was careful not to be seen going in and out but there wasn't much that he missed in the village. After all that was what he was paid for. The families involved did not object so he let it pass. Jessie was a quiet little thing and not likely to cause any trouble for the new owner or the villagers. Sighing, he reached for his empty cup and headed for the coffee machine. Wonderful this modern machine he thought. At least the village had decided to keep up with the times so all the luxuries of today were at his disposal. Hearing a key in the door he headed for the outer office and the beginning of his day. May it please be an easy one he thought. Pushing his chair back under the desk he made his way to the door and into the hall. The day was started.

— CHAPTER 27 —

Rachel left the real estate office with a happy skip. The papers were finally signed and the store was hers. It had taken some time to persuade Mr. Johnson but in the end he really had no excuse not to let her have it. She was after all paying the full price asked and with cash at that. She was a bit surprised to find that to purchase it she had to agree to keep the shop girl that worked for the previous owner. Mr. Johnson assured her that it was for a one year period only and if things did not work out during that time she could cancel the contract.

On rethinking it she decided that the girl might not be a bad idea as she would not only know the business but the customers as well. As she left Mr. Johnson's office the world looked good. She stepped out the door and looking up the street she started on a new era in her life.

Jessie finished sweeping out the store. She figured the new owner should at least see a clean floor when she arrived. Mr. Johnson had come to see her the day before to tell her about the new owner and what would be happening to her. Mr. Johnson had always known she was staying at the store and had not stopped her as he felt she would work very well as an unpaid caretaker.

It was to be kept a secret from the rest of the village as most of them thought that Jessie had moved on and were more than happy for it. She still carried the stigma of her family, who in the past were not thought of well in the village. Not descendants that you would hang pictures on the wall or look up in the village historical files. Still as long as she had worked for Rebecca she had been tolerated. Now that the new owner was also taking her on they would have to suck it up.

She set the broom in the corner and glanced back over the living quarters. Her bed was made and there were no dirty dishes in the sink. She had polished the wooden table until it shone and the white breezy curtains hung in soft folds. Yes, she smiled everything looked fine.

Suddenly she realized this was now officially her place and she wouldn't have to sneak in and out ever again. Checking her hair in the mirror over the sink she was actually smiling, something she hadn't done in some time. A rattling at the front door brought her sharply out of her thoughts. It was time to make an impression on the new owner. She hoped the woman would be kind as Rebecca had been. She missed Rebecca as she had been the closest thing to family Jessie had ever known. There had never been toys or games in her life. Her life had just begun when Rebecca took her in and now she was gone.

One final look told her that all was well and she could relax now that the shop was sold. A sound from the front door bell told her that her life was finally going to begin. She made her way to the front, smile on her face ready to face the day.

CHAPTER 28

Rachel pulled up in front of her house. She glanced over at the girl at her side. She had been very quiet on the drive from the village and Rachel wondered if this had been a bad idea after all. She had hoped that talking to Jessie about their arrangement at the house would make her more at home in her new life. So she stopped at the store on her way home from the real estate office to pick her up and look over her new purchase.

She was surprised to find the girl Jessie ready and wondered if Mr. Johnson had called ahead or if she was already there. The first trip to the store she had the uncanny feeling that someone was there but there was no real evidence of it at the time. Now on second look she realized it was just a bit too tidy for a store left vacant for five years. Not enough dust and a bit too comfortable. Well not that it mattered; it would just mean that nothing would be neglected too badly.

She reached over and touched the girls arm and smiling opened her door and stepped from the car. Making her way to the other side of the car she opened Jessie's door and waited for her to step out. Jessie was awed at the sight of the house in front of her. She had always heard about this house but had never ventured out to see it. It was the most beautiful place she had ever seen.

Both sides of the house were covered with blossoms and she caught the fragrance from both as they intertwined in the soft breeze. She stood looking at the massive front door and even with the warm summer breeze she felt a slight shiver up her spine. Noticing that Jessie was hesitating Rachel took her arm and steered her towards the house. Climbing the front steps she reached forward and unlocked the door and they entered the front hall.

Inside the door Jessie stopped dead in her tracks. If she wasn't frightened before she was the minute she entered the hall. The smell of roses was so overpowering that she nearly dropped to her knees. The bright sun they had just come in from was gone and had been replaced by a heavy dusk. Jessie grasped the door handle behind her and leaned against the door.

Glancing at Rachel just ahead of her she suddenly realized that Rachel was not seeing the same thing she was. Certainly she would have to be seeing the wallpaper in the hall with its many roses and lilacs intertwined. To Jessie they seemed alive. Looking at Rachel she could see that the area Rachel stood in was not dark as hers but sunny as if she still stood on the porch. As she reached out to Rachel suddenly everything changed and she was back once more in the sunshine.

Rachel turned to find Jessie leaning against the front door with her hand extended towards her. She had turned pale and Rachel could see she was very frightened. She started towards her. What on earth could have happened to make her look this way? Perhaps she had twisted her ankle she thought moving towards the girl.

Just as she reached her Jessie slipped slowly to the floor in a dead faint. Rachel reached down and lifting her took her to the nearby parlour and sat her on the couch just inside the door. Then she hurried to the kitchen for water and a cold cloth. As she left the room once more there was a strong smell of roses and lilacs. It wafted like a breeze down the stairway and into the parlour closing the door behind.

Rachel decided she had to do something about her imagination. She had never been much for seeing things that weren't there, but since arriving in the village life did not seem as simple or as easy as it had been this far in her life. She would have to do something about this. She settled Jessie on the couch and headed for the kitchen and a cold cloth.

— CHAPTER 29 —

Dan drove by the empty store on Main Street. He knew the old house had a new owner and had just recently heard that its owner had also purchased the empty shop in town. No one had paid much attention to the shop since the past owner died and were quite content to see it sit empty. Forever if necessary.

There had been whispering about what was happening in the bookstore/gift shop. Some of the men in the village had forbidden their wives to shop there. The owner a quiet old soul had not been considered harmful but there had been whisperings of potions being made for the ladies to keep them young. Nothing more than fancy soap or colourful lotions were ever displayed but it had always been rumoured that Rebecca kept other potions on hand in her backrooms.

Jessie, her shop girl also delivered to homes on the outskirts of the village after the shop was closed each day. Still nothing had been found out of order and when Rebecca died the sheriff had simply locked the door. He wondered what had become of Jessie as no one had really seen her since the store closed. Once in a while she had been noticed coming out of the grocers but then she seemed to just disappear. He decided he would have to look her up as she might be able to shed some light on the new owner.

Dave Johnson had told him that there was a clause in the lease saying that the new owner would have to employ Jessie when they purchased it so he imagined that Dave knew where to reach her. He pulled over to the side of the road two doors down the street and checked out the store from a distance. It looked surprisingly clean for a store that had stood empty for five years. He was sure that the front windows, although they were covered with paper had been freshly washed. Also, the front stoop had definitely just been swept.

Startled by a car pulling in ahead of him he moved lower in the seat to be less noticeable. He watched as a tall fair haired woman stepped from the driver's side and approached the store. Just as she reached the door it opened and Jessie stepped out. Jessie was already in the store. Could this be where she had been living for the past five years? How could this have gone unnoticed?

Dan thought over the layout of the small bookstore and wondered how no one would know of her presence. True if she wanted to use it as a hideout so to speak she would only have to be quiet during the daytime when the other shops were open. After five every evening the other shops were closed and there were no residents on the street. Also, he knew that the only shops on the street with windows at the back belonged to Josh Stewart, the barber and Jack Simmons, the butcher who had added to the back of the buildings and installed windows at the time. So it would be quite simple to live there without anyone being aware.

He watched as Jessie climbed into the car and they drove away. Putting his car in gear he slowly followed them through the village to the old road leading to the Warren house. Dan followed them until they turned off the main road. Pulling over to the side of the road he sat for a few minutes listening to the quiet around him. So this was the new owner he mused and Jessie was being given the inside track with her. Well it looked like it was time to spend a little time with Jessie he thought smiling. There might still be a chance for him after all. Starting the car he pulled slowly away and continued up the road toward home.

— CHAPTER 30 —

Rachel was tired. She had spent all day at the shop with Jessie. She had decided that after the spell Jessie had the night before at the house that she must be run down and would need help setting up the store for business. She had dropped her off at the store telling her to stay there overnight and that she would be back the next morning to help. Now she was bone tired as there had been more to do than had met the eye on her first visit.

The covers on the window had blocked out the fact that most of the dust was still there from the time Rebecca died. The living quarters were in fair shape but the store itself had needed a good scrubbing. Most of the stock could be salvaged except for a few books that had been destroyed from a small leak in the roof. The leak had been repaired sometime over the five year period the store had been empty but the damaged goods had been left to mold. So the day had been a tiring one.

She left Jessie to finish up and came home for a hot bath and cup of tea. Throwing her coat over the kitchen chair she went to the sink to fill the kettle. The kitchen was stuffy from being closed up all day so she reached over and opened the window over the sink. A slight breeze moved the curtains and wafted the fragrance of lilacs into the kitchen. Rachel stood with the kettle still in her hand breathing in the wonderful fragrance. It was almost hypnotic. Setting the kettle back on the cupboard she turned away from the sink.

It was then she noticed the door to the root cellar was slightly ajar. She was sure she had checked the kitchen before going out this morning and the door had been closed. It was unusual having a door to the root cellar from the inside of the house as well as the outside and it had made her just a bit nervous. Because of this she always checked to make sure the inside one was closed when she left the house.

Walking to the door she peeked around to see if there was a light on below. Since there wasn't she reached around the door and turned it on. A dim light came from the single bulb at the bottom of the stairs. Calling down she suddenly felt rather foolish as who could possibly be down there to answer. This was the one area she had not checked yet so she decided there was no better time than now to do so.

Making her way slowly down the steps she found herself in one large room lined on both sides with deep vegetable bins. To the back were two large closets with heavy locks and a long table obviously used for sorting things in their proper place. She walked over to the cupboards and fingered the heavy locks. There wasn't any evidence of keys so she began searching for something to break the locks.

In the corner she found a sledgehammer and a rusty crowbar. One of these should work she thought. Carrying them back to the cupboards she proceeded to hammer at the first lock. They were very old and the first swing of the hammer dropped the lock to the floor. The door swung open revealing nothing more than old clothes and broken china. Nothing here she thought. Perhaps the second one would reveal something more interesting.

This lock did not give up as easily and it took both the hammer and the crowbar to finally break it loose. Once again old clothes on one shelf but the other shelf held several old books. There were a few novels mostly and one or two history books. Then on moving them aside she found something of more interest. Tucked away in the corner was a small much worn leather journal. When she opened it she found it was written in a very delicate hand.

She thought it might have belonged to her cousin Karen but the name she found was Bridgett. The last name was smudged and she was unable to make it out. Suddenly she felt very tired. Tucking the journal in her pocket she gathered up the local history books and closed the cupboard. This would give her reading material for tonight after her bath. She made her way up the stairs and turned out the light. Closing the door once again she went to the sink to fill the kettle for her tea.

CHAPTER 31

Jessie dropped down on the kitchen chair and kicked off her shoes. As she looked back on the day she realized it had been a good one. The shop fairly sparkled and really could be opened tomorrow if Rachel wanted. They had talked about this but since it was Friday and the shop would be closed Sunday they decided to wait till the first of the week for the opening.

She stretched her arms over her head and looked around the living quarters. Her living quarters. This part of her dream had finally come true. Her own place. There hadn't been too much to do as she had been living here for some time and kept it to suit herself. She was surprised that Rachel hadn't questioned her about where she had been staying and why the living quarters were so clean and the rest of the shop in such poor condition. It didn't matter as the place was hers and she could come and go right out in the open.

She was just about to pour her tea when she heard a knock on the front door of the shop. Checking the clock she found it wasn't as late as she thought it had been so it was logical she might have a visitor. There was always a chance that Rachel had forgotten something and since they hadn't made a second set of keys yet there was no way for her into the shop without Jessie letting her in. Making her way to the front of the store she peeked around the blind on the door. To her surprise it was not Rachel but Dan. She knew Dan only slightly from seeing him in the village. He had never been a visitor to the store and she wondered why he was coming now. She slipped the lock off and slowly opened the door.

Dan watched Jessie peek around the blind before opening the door. He wondered how he would approach her. After talking with Jack Simmons and Josh Stewart he knew he would be the one to find out what was going on in the empty shop. Now that he was here he wondered how to go about it.

"Jessie, how nice to see you around again. We all thought you had moved from the area after Rebecca died and now we find you have been here all along. You must bring me up to date with what is happening to the shop and all about the new owner."

He slowly eased the door handle out of Jessie's hand and moved into the dim shop. Backing her up into the shop he closed the door behind him and turned the lock. Jessie back away from him towards her living quarters where the lighting seemed more friendly than the dim one in the shop. She felt a slight shiver as she realized that Dan was following her.

Suddenly she was aware of the strong fragrance of violets. Everything around her seemed to be transparent as if in a fog. She put both hands on a nearby table to steady herself and as she did she felt someone take hold of both arms and pull her away. Suddenly she was falling and just as the darkness spread over her, she heard the voice of a woman calling out to her. Before she could make out the words she was aware of someone shaking her.

Jessie opened her eyes to the sight of Dan holding her head. There was a look of concern on his face and she wondered what was troubling him. Then as it had started the fragrance of violets was gone and her eyesight cleared. Now she was more aware of Dan holding her and tried to move away.

"Don't be in a hurry to move," he said. "You hit your head on the table as you fell and it looks like you may have quite a bruise." Jessie put her hand to her head and for the first time was aware of a slight pain there.

"What happened?" she asked. "Did I trip over something on the floor?" "No," Dan replied. "You just seemed to lose consciousness for no reason that I could see. Perhaps you are just over tired with all the work you have been doing in the shop. That was the reason for my visit. I was going to invite you and the new owner for dinner as I'm sure you have been skipping real meals for the past few days." Jessie was aware that she was still being held by Dan and suddenly felt very uncomfortable. Easing her way out of his arms she pulled herself to her feet and leaned against the nearby table. True they had been missing meals with all the work to be done and she was just about to do something about it when Dan came to the door. She remembered she had just put the kettle on when she heard a knock.

Not knowing how long she had been out she excused herself to see if she indeed still had a kettle or if the bottom had burned out. When she entered the kitchen she found the kettle still in one piece. So she hadn't been out very long. As she turned to go back into the shop she found that Dan had followed her into the kitchen. A shiver went down her spine and she realized that she was more than a little uncomfortable with him. "Everything fine," he asked? "Yes," she replied as she turned the kettle off.

"Fine," Dan replied. "Then there is no reason for you not to accept my dinner invitation." Jessie felt a slight pang of something. Was it fear? Why should that be, she hardly knew Dan. She remembered he had been seeing the former owner of the house that her new employer had inherited. She had seen him around the village, but that was about the extent of knowing him. He was a well-respected member of the village but not in her class. So, she wondered why he would want to be seen with her, a shop girl. He did say he was coming to ask both herself and her new employer so maybe when he found she was the only one there he was simply being polite in an awkward situation.

Yes, that would be it she thought. Well the offer was still there regardless and she did have to eat, so why not. Smiling at Dan she said, "I will accept the invitation if it's still open."

Dan reached out and took her coat from the back of the chair and held it out to her. Well, she thought I guess it still is. Slipping her arms into her coat she checked to be sure all the burners were off on the stove and made her way to the door. Dan slipped his hand under her elbow and steered her towards the front. He was glad that he was a step or two behind her as she was unable to see the look of satisfaction on his face at being able to reach his goal so easy. He was sure he would have no trouble finding out the information he needed about the new owner. He took the key from Jessie's hand and slowly locked the door behind them. Leaving the scent of violets fading into the shop.

— CHAPTER 32 —

Edna had been at the window for over an hour, just watching. Joe was late this morning. She couldn't remember when this had happened before as she could nearly set the clocks by his arrival. She pulled back the lace curtains and glanced upwards at the windows next door. Yes, they were watching too. This was just one more change in the house.

Suddenly a movement at the back of the house drew her attention. She quickly dropped the curtain and moved back into the room. She wasn't quite sure what she had seen. The movement had been so slight she wasn't sure if she had seen it at all. It may have been only a shadow. No, there it was again and this time she was sure there was a figure standing at the outside door to the basement. She thought for a moment it was Joe until she realized Joe's old truck was just pulling up the drive. Looking back she found the figure had disappeared.

She turned her attention back to Joe who was unloading his tools in preparation for another day in the garden. She settled herself in her chair by the window to watch Joe tend the roses on her side of the house. He had never had much tending here as the roses seemed to have a life of their own. Each morning when she opened the curtains she was sure they had grown overnight. She lifted a hand in greeting and Joe answered with a nod.

They had known each other for many years and Joe had been the only gardener. He looked after all the beds and from time to time loosened the soil around the roses. This was all the roses needed. Each morning they were thicker than the day before and now they had spread across the back of the house where they were met by towering lilac bushes. She couldn't remember when the lilac bushes had come as she knew Joe hadn't planted them. They too needed very little tending. Still both added to the appearance of the house. Once more she glanced toward the outside cellar door. All seemed quiet there now.

Joe took his old bandana from his back pocket and wiped his brow. He stood looking over the gardens, his gardens. This was how he thought of them. He didn't care that much about the house. It was also his job to make sure the cleaning crew was there once a month to keep the inside clean, which he did without fail. However, the gardens were his. He had never been in the house. The last owner had invited him in but he had declined. There was something about the house that kept him away. Whatever it was he was content to just work in his garden and leave the rest of the house alone. As he moved along the side of the house the fragrance from the flowers swirled around him wafting up to the second floor windows to disappear into the mist behind them.

— CHAPTER 33 —

Jack parked his car to the side of the road and turned out the lights. He knew there was something going on at the old Warren house. After a meeting with Dan and Josh it had been decided that one of them should find their way into the house to see what they could find. Dan had become friends with the last owner and for a while thought that he would be buying the house. The owner at that time had just come to settle her fathers' estate, which included the Warren house.

However, after arriving she decided she was going to stay and put down roots so the house was taken off the market. Things were moving on well for him until Karen had travelled back to her previous home to collect her things and had never returned. So the house sat empty again. A fund had been set up by Karen's father to care for the house and gardens, and as there was still money in the account things went on as usual.

The house had always been considered bewitched as during the witch scares it was rumoured one had lived there and had left their mark for future residents. Years before during the witch hunts the village had decided that no outsider would be allowed to live in the village, thereby keeping all witches at bay. This was a well-kept secret by everyone in the village. So when a new face appeared the village committee knew they would have to see if anything was going on in the old Warren house.

He stepped around the back of the house to the old outside door to the root cellar. He knew there was an inside door to the basement, so if he could gain access from the outside he would only have to mount the steps to the inside door. With luck Joe wasn't in the garden yet. He knew this might be his only setback as he couldn't get in with Joe in the yard. If Joe was there he had planned on telling him that his car had broken down out on the highway and ask to use the phone. But as luck would have it Joe was having a late morning leaving the house free for Jack to enter.

As he reached down to open the basement door something caused him to look toward the house next door. He was sure he saw the window curtains flutter. He stepped back quickly out of sight just in time as a truck pulled up the lane. Peeking around the corner he checked once again on the window and satisfied that there was no movement he pulled open the door and disappeared into the dark below.

— CHAPTER 34 —

Josh started to turn the key in the door of his shop. It was the beginning of another week. He glanced at the shop next door and was surprised that everything was still closed. Usually Jack was either in the shop or at his front door the same time every morning as he was. He stepped over to the front door of the butcher shop and peered through the window. All was quiet. No light from the back suggesting Jack had come in early to set things up for the day.

Something was wrong. In all the years both men had never missed a day in their shops or for that matter been late. He turned back and slipped the key into the lock of his own shop and entered. It was Monday and he knew he would not be busy as most of his customers were in on Friday and Saturday to spruce up for the weekend. These days usually turned out to be more like social gatherings as this is when everyone caught up on the local gossip.

He reached over and turned on the lights and began to assess the days' work. Everything would have a good cleaning and stock would be ordered today. He went to the door and glanced once more at the shop next door. Still no movement. Something was wrong. He would open the shop and then give Jack a call at home to see what the problem was. Switching on the lights he reached for the broom and began opening for the day.

— CHAPTER 35 —

Jack hurriedly pulled the door to the basement closed behind him. He heard the creak of old wood as it slipped into place over his head. He supposed this door hadn't been used much since the one had been installed inside the house. When the house was new it had been the only access to the basement which served just as a root cellar for the garden vegetables and fruit grown on the land. Today there was no vegetable garden and the fruit trees had been cut down long ago.

Such a shame that so many of the old ways had been left in the past. Not so with village beliefs he thought and was thankful for that. He stood quietly for a few minutes not wanting to be heard by anyone from above. He knew Joe was just there to check out the next week's work before leaving for his typical trip to the coffee shop to gossip with his friends.

He heard Joe pass above him and pause at the basement door. He found he was barely breathing as the door handle above him rattled at Joes' touch. He was caught. Then just as fast as it had been touched the handle slipped back into place and footsteps moved away. Letting his breath go Jack felt his heart slowly dropping into normal beating once more and he slid down the wall to sit on the steps. For another twenty minutes he sat there until finally he heard the sound of Joe's truck fading down the drive. He was gone for the day.

Standing he slowly made his way to the bottom of the stairs. Reaching up he pulled the string to the single light bulb attached to the ceiling. The basement seemed almost like someone had just dug a hole in the ground and put a door on top. Because of this the ceiling was very low and Jack had to walk in a stooped manner until he was nearly to the centre of the room. When he was finally able to stand upright he looked over the contents. What had once been a very functional food cellar now held only empty wooden crates and baskets from the past. Dust and cobwebs covered everything except one small corner that seemed to have escaped. Here he found a small wooden trunk pushed behind a small table and rather well-kept rocking chair. The table held a quite modern lamp and there was evidence of this area being recently used. Why that sly old fox, Jack chuckled. So many of the hours Joe put in for wages were spent down here where no one would know. Still smiling he reached for the small chest and pulled it toward him.

The lock seemed fairly new and all evidence showed it had been opened recently. It wasn't stiff or rusted as it should be for having been stored in such a damp unused place. He reached into his pocket for his pen knife and proceeded to work on the lock. It took just a few minutes and the lock slipped open. Pushing open the top Jack found the chest empty except for a small journal nestled at the bottom. Jack carefully lifted it. It seemed very old and fragile. Carefully opening it to the first page he found in almost indistinct writing the name Bridgett O'Hara.

With a jolt Jack dropped into the rocking chair still clasping the journal in his shaking hand. He sat for a moment, thoughts swirling in his head. This was it he thought. The stories about a hidden journal were true. The history of the house and the village. For many years the story had been told like an old folk tale as part of the history. Children had been told while very young that the Warren House was haunted and that they should never go near it. Old Joe had kept the story alive to keep the local children of each generation out of his prized garden. It had worked for the most part until finally the fun of it wore off and other things took over in the children's minds.

However, for most of the older folks the stigma still remained and the house was left to its' own. As it remained privately owned by one family there had been no need for anyone to go there except Joe, who was the official caretaker, and the cleaning crew that the estate paid to come in monthly to keep the property in good shape. The only resident near was old Edna next door. Both Edna and Joe were almost ageless.

Now looking down at the journal once again the stories of the past swirled around in Jack's mind. He remembered one story that was a bit more personal to his family and to that of Josh. It involved a woman named Nora something or other. He couldn't remember her last name. The only thing he did remember was somehow she was connected to this house and it was something he wasn't to talk about. Not that he could for he didn't really know anything.

The most he and Josh could ever find out was eavesdropping on the conversations of their parents from behind closed doors. This had been a real adventure for them when they were young but soon fishing and girls had taken over and they left the stories in the past. Quite where they belonged Jack thought.

Sitting back in the chair he opened the journal and started to read. Time seemed to stand still as Jack got further into what he found was not only the history of the house but the history of the village. The first entries seemed to be made by Bridgett. The owner of the journal. He found entries by Nora and from someone named Karen. From the faded writing it looked like there were several years between these entries. Taking a small notebook from his pocket he entered all the names with the idea of looking them up in the town history. Some of them, particularly Nora were rather brutal.

Adjusting his position in the chair to ease the pain in his back he realized he had been sitting in the basement for a long time. He may have been missed by now and his car had been parked on the road long enough for it to be questioned by at least one of the locals. He made a few more notes then carefully slipped the journal back into the chest and once more secured the lock. He wanted to take it with him but something at the last minute told him to leave it where it was.

He knew that he could get into the basement any Sunday as no one was around on this day. Maybe next time he would bring Josh and they might be able to figure it out together. They had always been able to solve problems since they were boys if they put their heads together, and he would also have the research on the names.

Slowly he stood up and stretched, stiff from sitting so long. He glanced at his watch and realized he had been in the basement for three hours. He would have some explaining to do when he got home. Just as he reached to turn off the light on the table all the lights went out. He stood transfixed as the air began to cool and the silence deepened. The strong smell of roses and lilacs filled the air and Jack found it very hard to breathe. Sudden panic filled him and it was then Jack realized he was not alone.

CHAPTER 36

Fred Baker had been driving through the streets of the village most of the morning. Sunday was always a quiet time as after the morning church service people left for home. There was nothing else to do except sit in the town square or the local soda fountain. Blakesville was a quiet village on Sunday. Not like the nearby Salem that hosted tourists all year long, no matter what the season, with their many stories of the past. Sunday was a day of rest and here in the village that was exactly the way it was.

Fred picked up a candy bar from the seat and pulled off the wrapper with his teeth. It was the main reason he liked being out touring the village as no one knew how many candy bars he ate so there was no one to nag him about it. He smiled to himself as he popped a piece of chocolate into his mouth. His one happy indulgence.

Circling around the square he decided he would take one sweep around the town before taking the car in for the day. It had been very uneventful. Not even a cat up a tree to attend to. Some people might find this kind of life boring, but not Fred.

He liked nothing better than to just drive around on his shift with candy bars at his side and the radio playing his kind of music with no one to say what he could or couldn't do.

Turning the car around he drove through the village to the road leading to the Warren House. Once again Fred laughed to himself. Maybe there was something doing at the haunted house of the village. He might even get a look at the ghosts said to be living there.

As he drove along the road towards the house he noticed Jack Simmonds car parked at the side of the road. Now this was a strange place to find Jack's car he thought. Pulling up behind the car he opened his door and got out. He looked the car over and not finding anything wrong with it or no one in the car he decided he would call in to see if maybe it was missing.

Reaching in his vehicle he pulled out his radio and proceeded to call. The static was so loud it hurt his ear and he dropped the unit to the seat. Once more he picked it up and tried to call the station. This time the noise was deafening and he turned it off and returned it to its holder. He made a note to have it looked at before the car went out on the road again and stepped back into the car, already forgetting why he was calling into the office to begin with.

He checked his watch and realized by the time he stopped off at the trash bin in the square to deposit all his candy wrappers it would be time to sign out for the day. He scribbled a note and stuck it to the dash of the police car for the mechanic about the radio noise and stepped into his own car. Putting it in gear he pulled away from the station and headed for home, Jack's car clearly out of his head.

CHAPTER 37

Sheriff Hennessey set his first morning coffee on the side of his desk. He noticed how quiet the village was on his way through this morning and hoped that was to be the pattern for the day. Not that much happened in the village any day, but today he hoped everyone would stay pretty much to home so he could catch up on the backload on his desk.

Each time this backload happened he promised himself it would be the last time but in spite of the promise he ended up with mountains of work to do in the end. He checked the roster to see who the duty man was and found it was himself.

With a sigh he settled down at his desk and waited for all hell to break loose as it usually did when he was alone. He shuffled the papers around on the desk hoping to start something not too complicated just in case. He had no more settled when the telephone rang. First one he thought as he picked it up. Laying back his chair and putting his feet on the desk he settled down for his first crisis of the day.

CHAPTER 38

The house was quiet this morning. Joe still hadn't arrived to tend the gardens so there was no noise from outside. Rachael had little time so far to spend at the house because of opening the new shop. She knew that Jessie was quite capable, probably more than herself, but she wanted her fingers in right at the beginning. Although Jessie would be the one to tend it mostly she wanted it clear to everyone that she was the owner. They spent the entire week-end together setting up the new cabinets and filling them with the new shipment of stock. Finally finished late last night she had headed for home and her bed.

Now after her morning tea she was ready to tackle something else and decided it would be in the house. The road coming home last night without light of any kind was very dark. She found herself leaning over the steering wheel to see her road. This as it happened was a good thing as someone had left their car parked to the side of the road just at her entrance. It seemed strange that it was still there at this hour and not towed in by the local garage. Still it was Sunday and the village held by the old ways of day of rest so it probably had to wait till this morning to be picked up. She had no idea who it might belong to as she wasn't familiar enough with folks as yet to know their vehicles.

She laughed to herself as she realized she had started using their way of speaking. She had never used the expression folks in her life. She was also sure she had never even heard it used. Now here she was falling into the lingo herself. Rinsing her cup in the sink she wondered what her first chore should be.

There were several areas of the house she hadn't visited yet, the basement, the attic and she was sure there were many closets with treasures that Karen or one of the other tenants had left behind. Since Karen had just lived in the house for such a short time it was more likely to be from someone in the past. She felt an excitement go through her at the thought of finding something from the history of the house.

She decided maybe the cellar first and reached for the door handle. A sudden chill ran up her arm and she dropped the handle back in place. There was something there. Rachel backed away into the kitchen still staring at the door. She half expected it to swing forward with all sorts of things spilling into the room. She stood still waiting but nothing happened. After a moment she decided she must just be overtired from the weekend work and once more approached the door. This time she took a good grasp on the handle and pulled. As the door opened the kitchen became very dark and a cold breeze filled the air. Rachel was unable to take her hand from the door handle. She stood transfixed at the change in her kitchen but was suddenly not afraid. She stood still holding the handle as a waft of fog like substance swirled up the staircase. It moved around the kitchen as if visiting an old friend and then came to settle just over Rachel's head. She felt a soft touch on her face and a quiet voice saying, "not yet". It circled her head once more then made its way down the stairs the voice still whispering, "Not yet, not yet," and it was gone. Rachel stood for a moment longer then closing the door behind her she left the room.

— CHAPTER 39 —

Jessie opened the front door of the shop for the first time on her own. She had hoped that Rachel would not leave her this soon. She knew that the house was just as important to Rachel as the shop and she hadn't too much time for it because they had been so busy. So she understood when Rachel said she wouldn't be in today. She took the polishing cloth from her pocket and polished off the door knob one more time. She turned and stood with her back to the door looking over the work they had done the past two days.

One side of the store was dedicated entirely to books. Rachel had purchased new shelves for this side and they had set up a small reading area with comfortable chairs and tiny tables. For today Rachel had also set up one end with a coffee machine and supplied little treats for any customer who wanted to linger. She wasn't sure if the treats would be continued after today but the coffee was to be permanent.

Starting at the front opposite the reading area were shelves of soaps and facial products along with sachets and lace handkerchiefs. There were small gift items that could be picked up at the last minute for forgotten birthday or anniversaries. To the back were the linens and hats and bolts of cloth for those interested in sewing. Rachel had also put in many fine threads and needles.

Just to the back behind the reading area was the cash counter. One end held a massive cash register while the other end was lined with large apothecary jars of peppermint, lemon drops, liquorice and horehound candy. Also at this end a small printed sign announced that special creams and fragrances could be ordered with one days' notice.

Jessie smiled at this as these were the special orders she had delivered for Rebecca when she was alive. Delivered at night so the men of the village would not be aware of them. Yes, she thought this was surely just a ladies shop. She moved away from the door just in time for the first two customers to arrive for the day. Turning she smiled and welcomed them not only to a new shop but to the first day of her new life.

— CHAPTER 40 —

Josh paced back and forth in front of his shop window. He had swept through and washed all the brushes and combs and was now ready for the day's work and still no Jack. Jack was never late and he wondered if he was ill. If so it must be serious as nothing kept Jack from work.

He remembered the time Jack had fallen on the ice getting out of his car and broken his leg. He had laid there until Josh arrived and then insisted he be taken into his shop to open up until his help arrived. Even with the pain in his leg he had managed to instruct Josh and another shop owner what had to be done to open up until he was relieved and taken to the doctor's. Nothing was more important than his shop.

He decided to wait another half hour then call Jack's wife. He hated to call her in case Jack had been in an accident and she hadn't been notified yet. So he would just have to pace for the moment until he heard. He noticed Dan crossing the road just above his store and thought possibly he might have some information. Opening the door he called out then waited for Dan to turn toward him, if anyone knew Dan would. Dan was pretty well engrossed in the business of the village so he had privy to everything that was happening. He stepped back inside and waited for Dan to arrive.

Dan turned as he heard his name called. He was surprised to find it was Josh and that Jack was not at his side. Since grade school the two had been shadows of one another. Even to the sweeping of the front walk at their stores they were inseparable. So the sight of Josh on his own worried Dan enough to make him retrace his steps and head for Josh's store. He noticed there was no movement in the butcher shop nor was there any evidence that anyone had been there yet. Not good he thought. There seemed to be something further up the street at Rebecca's old shop. Then he remembered the girl who had inherited the Warren house had also bought the empty store two doors down. Out front was a large sign covered with balloons and streamers that read grand opening. Well, she hadn't wasted any time establishing herself in the village. Once he settled with Josh he would have to take a run down and see just what kind of shop she had opened.

He had befriended Jessie, the shop girl but at that point she had very little to tell him except she would be working there and living behind the shop. She had seemed very excited about the whole thing and he had promised himself he would look into it soon. Best to make sure it was the right kind of shop this time.

He opened the door to the barbershop to the sad face of Josh sitting in one of his barber chairs. He walked over and sat in the other chair and prepared himself for what Josh was now considering important enough to haul him in off the street first thing Monday morning.

CHAPTER 41

Edna's hand shook as she released her curtain once more into place. She had seen the fog settling around the house next door and knew that what she had feared was indeed happening. Since Karen had left everything had been quiet and Edna hoped that for at least now in her lifetime things were over. The years she had been watching had been hard ones. She had seen things she didn't care to remember. She had watched as the stigma of the village claimed the souls from this house.

Edna was old, much older than most and very tired. She and Joe had been made responsible for the Warren house and they carried out their duties well. Back at the beginning everything seemed to go in order. The village weeded out anything or anyone that did not fit in their plan. Then a young couple, who were not from the village, came to live in the house. They weren't more than just children and newlywed. She remembered how excited the girl was at having her own place and how hard she tried to fit in. Everything seemed to be working out well until the fateful evening of her first dinner party. From that day on nothing had been the same.

She had heard rumours of witchcraft and people disappearing mysteriously in the house but she had been told nothing and dared not ask. It was just a week later that Bridgett had suddenly decided to return to her parents' house leaving her new husband behind. He had become a recluse after she left and a few weeks later he too was gone.

There had been no movers or any evidence of anything being taken away from the house so she assumed everything was still there. At one point a man and his wife had come to stay for a few days. They too left everything as it was and one morning left, leaving a for sale sign on the front lawn. However, the house had never sold and a tiny shiver went down her spine as she realized it never would. With a final peek at the upstairs window next door she retreated to her chair and waited for her house girl to bring her lunch.

— CHAPTER 42 —

Rachel stood looking out the small window in the front door. She wondered how she had arrived in the front hallway. She had just finished her morning tea and rinsed her cup in the kitchen sink. She didn't remember leaving the kitchen. She remembered thinking that she would spend today just checking out the house. She had pretty much checked out the downstairs but since buying the little shop on Main Street she had been busy there and the house had been set aside. She stood for a moment longer then turning made her way up the stairs.

She followed closely to the banister on the way up as she had experienced a strange sensation if she walked too close to the rose wallpaper. She could always smell the roses in the hallway but climbing the stairs it was as if she were entering a rose garden. It was then that the roses seemed to overpower her and was very frightening. Silly as it seemed she found it much safer to walk close to the banister until she reached the top. Now standing at the end of the hallway the smell of roses faded and she felt more secure.

Looking down the hall she took stock of the rooms on the second floor. To her right were two bedrooms. The first one she had chosen on the night she arrived. Not for any reason except it was the closest and her bags were getting heavy. A fast peek in told her that the one next to her was also a bedroom as was the one directly across from it. The room across from hers was the bathroom and these two rooms were separated by a small door she had not tried yet.

She remembered looking in the one next to hers and finding it although clean nothing out of the ordinary. Unlike the one she chose that continued on the rose theme from the hall. She had thought of changing her room to the one next to hers but never seemed to find the time to make the change. The one across the hall had been locked and until now she had not been able to find the key. This left the small door in between the bathroom and the locked room.

This might just be the time to do some exploring she thought and moving forward took hold of the small brass knob on the door. There seemed to be some resistance and she had to turn it two or three times before the door opened to a musty staircase. The attic, of course. She had noticed a small window at the front of the house the day she arrived but had thought little of it since. Attics were usually a place of hidden treasures so this could turn out to be an exciting day.

Making her way up the narrow staircase she was unaware of the door closing quietly behind her. Had she been she might have backed down the few steps she had already taken. At the top she found one dingy room with some light from the small window to her left. The window also was covered with many years of dust and was letting in very little light. There must be a light somewhere she thought looking around. Yes, there hanging from the ceiling she found one small light bulb hanging from a single wire with a string attached. Reaching up she pulled the string filling the room with light. Even with the light there were still gloomy corners and Rachel could see outlines of some sort.

She made her way to the one on her left closest to the window and found a large old fashioned trunk. The lid to the trunk was open and except for a few pieces of cloth and a black teacup it was empty. Disappointed at not finding the treasures she hoped for she turned to the corner at the back. Once more she found a huge trunk but this one was locked. Annoyed with herself for not bringing at least a screwdriver and a flashlight she dropped to the floor and began working at the lock. It too was old fashioned, very much like the door knob to the attic stairs. Someone had taken the trouble to design an ornate pattern for both of them. Somewhere in her mind she remembered seeing this pattern, but could not remember where.

She was just about to drop the lock and give up for the day when suddenly it fell open in her hand. She sat very still for a moment. She knew she had done nothing to release it and here it was old and rusty yet free in her hand. Not possible. Lifting the latch, the trunk top slowly creaked open revealing its contents to her. This one unlike the other contained many articles. Making herself more comfortable on the floor she began unpacking the contents. The first thing that caught her eye was another black teacup. She wondered if the rest of the set might be in this trunk. If so she would take them downstairs for herself. You never knew in a small town when you might have neighbours drop in and she could use them to entertain.

Setting it aside she dug further into the trunk. It turned out what was left was mostly books and papers. She would have to pull them out later to see what the connection might be with her ancestors, but for the moment she would pass. Just as she was closing the trunk lid a small journal caught her eye. The unusual thing about it was that she could see a picture on the cover. No not a picture, it was more like a photo taken of two young women.

Reaching in she managed to pull it from the trunk just as the lid closed. There was something familiar about the one woman she thought. They were both very attractive but seemed from different eras. One was dressed in more modern dress, not too many years ago while the other was in old fashioned dress of at least a century before. They sat side by side on an old settee holding hands smiling at the camera. The background looked familiar like it could be somewhere in the house.

Rachel felt a sudden chill and looking around felt that she was not alone. The room filled with the smell of roses and lilacs. She knew she had to get out of the attic right away. As she moved to the staircase the overhead light went out and her fear grew in the darkness. Cautiously she moved down the steps to the door. The door was closed. She knew she had left it open when she came up, yet now it was closed. As she reached for the knob the door suddenly opened and the light of the hall shone through. She tumbled down the stairs and rushed for the staircase to the lower level. Just as she put her foot on the top step the door to the attic closed once again and in the distance there was the metal sound of an old fashioned lock closing.

— CHAPTER 43 —

Josh sat patiently across the desk from Sheriff Hennessey. He had called Jack's house earlier this morning to find that Jack had not come home last night. His wife had not seen him since church when he left to do some work at the store. This was news to Josh, who knew Jack's every move. They had stopped at the coffee shop as usual after church and as far as Josh knew they had both struck out for home and their Sunday meal.

There had been no mention of anything being done at the shop. They had spoken in detail about their families particularly their grandfathers who had some sort of scandal connected to them. The families kept it to themselves but over the years the men had picked up enough here and there to put two and two together and come up with hints of witchcraft. It was only recently however, that they had decided to really delve into the past and see what was being hidden. Now Jack had disappeared. How much was connected he wondered.

Sheriff Hennessey put the phone down and turned to look at Josh's worried face. He was sure that there was nothing to worry about but after looking at Josh he decided he better at least show an effort at doing something. Pushing back in his chair he invited Josh to tell him all he knew about Jack's movements the day before.

CHAPTER 44

Sheriff Hennessey locked the door to his office and picked up his jacket from the hall. The call he had taken while Josh was in the office had been from Rachel, the new owner of the Warren house and the gift shop on Main Street. She was calling to report a car left overnight at her front gate. From her description it sounded very much like the car that Jack drove. He hesitated to tell Josh until he was sure that the car did belong to Jack, as Josh was in bad enough shape as it was. He dropped off the duty roster and the report of the car with the man at the desk, ordering a pick-up of the car and left the office.

He would be spending the next hour or more at the library. There had always been hints that both families had been involved in witch trials. This on its own might not be much as most of the village had at one time or another been involved. It was because of the beliefs that the village kept newcomers from living there. Only the blood descendants of the original villagers were allowed to purchase land and everyone else was considered a visitor and gently if possible invited to leave.

The sheriff waved a hand at the girl behind the desk that served as the librarian's throne. He knew his way well enough. He had spent many hours in the back room looking for information on one case or another. He sat down in front of the monitor and turned it on. He wasn't sure what year he was looking for but decided to start in the 1800's when witches were most widely known. He also wasn't sure why he thought that witches might be involved with things that had recently happened in the village. Still it was a place to start.

The history of witchcraft was long and wordy so after an hour he decided to check the local papers of more recent years. Starting with the oldest he worked his way through some of the trials of the village. He knew many young women had been convicted with very little evidence of their guilt. Many of the village women who were holding grudges against their neighbours of friendships gone sour had pointed their finger condemning them to death. It had gone on for many weeks until finally the sheriff at that time had called a halt and ordered any accused sent to Boston to be tried by another court. This seemed to end the trials and everything fell back into some sort of normal.

As he worked his way through the papers two names suddenly came up, Jack Simmons and Josh Stewart. He stopped the film and began to read. The story was about a young teacher, Nora Preston who had been wrongly accused of being a witch by the wives of both men. On the prodding from their wives they had taken the young woman from her home and without a trial had her burned at the stake in the Town Square.

When the women had confessed to just being angry at the marks their daughters had received on their last reports the village sheriff decided to put an end to any further trials in the village. This had to be the ancestors of Jack and Josh. Sheriff Hennessey felt a shiver down his spine. It couldn't be happening again could it? Closing the screen he made his way across the library and out the front door. He would look into the deserted car himself.

— CHAPTER 45 —

Jessie sat back and dropped her shoes on the floor. She was sure her feet had never hurt this much in her whole life. Not that she was complaining, it had been a wonderful day. People were coming and going for most of the day and she had barely time to refill the coffee pot. Rachel had called in earlier and asked if she thought she could handle the shop alone as she wanted to catch up on some work at the house.

She had said yes, but had not been prepared for the onslaught she received after she opened the door in the morning. She wasn't about to call Rachel and tell her she couldn't handle things so she plodded through the best she could until she could close the door. All she wanted to do now was sit back with a hot cup of tea and rest her tired feet.

Suddenly a knock at the door brought her back to reality. Slipping her shoes back on she made her way through the store and peeked around the blind. She was about to call out we're closed when she realized it was Dan smiling at her. Lifting the lock she opened the door just enough to acknowledge him. Not tonight she thought shifting from one tired foot to another, I just want to go to bed.

Realizing he wasn't going to go away she opened the door wider and invited him into the shop. Dan pushed the door closed behind him. He wondered if he could persuade Jessie to tell him about Rachel's plans. At first he thought he might get closer to Rachel herself but he realized it might be easier to approach Jessie as she knew him from the village.

He had never had any problems with women and Jessie seemed like quite an innocent. More of a pushover than Rachel might be coming from the city. He had hoped for more time but now that Jack was missing he had to move the plan ahead some. He needed to know about the house. It could not go back to the family. The village depended on it staying empty. Before he left here tonight he would know.

He followed Jessie up through the shop noting as he went how clean everything looked for a shop closed up this long. It was as if Rebecca were still here dusting and polishing as she had while she was alive. The whole place had a lived in feeling about it. He watched Jessie moving ahead touching and straightening things as she went, as if it was just another ordinary day in her life.

He had the feeling there was more to this little shop than met the eye. He also wondered where Jack was. Once more he realized that the men of the village needed to take hold of things to keep the old ways from coming back. Ahead Jessie stood at the door to the living quarters and he wondered what might be sealed behind these doors.

— CHAPTER 46 —

Rachel found herself sitting at the bottom of the attic stairs. She didn't remember being in the attic or even coming to the second floor. The last memory was putting her teacup in the rack to dry and turning toward the basement door. She didn't remember falling but checked everywhere to make sure she had no injuries and reached for the doorknob above her head. Grasping it firmly she pulled herself to her feet.

She remembered thinking how tidy the attic seemed for a house vacant for such a long time. Attics to her had always been a place of hidden treasures. There was always enough of the past there to keep her occupied for at least several days. She remembered as a child going through box after box of her grandparents things with such joy. There were always old clothes she could try on and pretend she was someone else besides herself. She always came away dusty clothes and skinned knees but smiling as she made her way down the stairs.

This one however, was neatly laid out and looking freshly dusted. She had found a few things, books and pictures of men and women in old style dress, yet nothing to hold attention for very long. Only the set of black dishes and candles that made her shiver at the touch. And of course, the little note book that would give her hours of reading later that night. Still it was not an ordinary attic. It held stories she wasn't sure she wanted to hear. Once again she was aware of sitting at the bottom of the stairs.

It was then the cold started. Pulling against it she found she couldn't release the door handle. Dropping the book she held, she placed her other hand on the handle and pulled harder. As she sank to her knees she was filled with the fragrance of violets and roses. It covered her like a blanket and she welcomed the feeling as she snuggled deeper into the dark. Soon there was no light at all. She was sure just at the end she heard the sound of clippers in the distance as the fragrance and the darkness overtook her.

— CHAPTER 47 —

Edna knew things were not going well. There had been too much movement at the windows next door in the past few days. Joe seemed to be going about his work as usual and that alone should make her feel secure but it didn't. The faces at the windows were becoming more clear. At first they had only been shadows but recently they had taken on a more solid look.

She dropped the curtain and walked over to the mantle. She picked up her fathers' pipe and held it close. If only he were here he would know what to do next. It had been so simple when her father was alive. When there were things to handle he just went ahead and looked after them. Now with him gone she was left to make all the decisions.

She stood for a few minutes gazing at her father's belongings before returning to the window and her watch. As she pulled the curtains she glanced towards the second floor windows of the house next door. A hand waved from the first window and the face of Bridgett O'Hara smiled down at her. She caught herself just about to wave back.

She remembered Bridgett when she first arrived in the village. She had been a young bride and so happy with her first home. She seemed like just the one to occupy the house. The village had talked long before they decided to bring Bridgett and her husband to the village. Jim worked for the company in another area and had proved himself to be an asset. They needed a replacement since one of the foremen had moved on and decided after much thought that Jim would fit the bill.

So Bridgett and Jim had come to Blakesville and the trouble had begun. At first Bridgett spent most of her time fixing up the house, so she didn't have time to join any of the ladies groups in the village. She and Jim attended church each Sunday and Jim became active in the local men's club. The men met every Wednesday night to discuss anything happening in the village that needed attending to. Usually it was nothing more than fixing a street light or repairing one of the local farmer's barns.

Still it was the duty of the men of the village to keep things in control and this they did well. It was also the duty of the men to decide who would be allowed to live in the village. Most of the village were descendants of the original families who had come from further south and were rumoured to be Quakers. This of course had not been established. The couple living in the house now were not related to or even known by the village. One meeting Edna remembered very well. It had been after a dinner party that Bridgett and Jim held not too long after their arrival. She remembered lights being on long into the night for a week before the party as Bridgett prepared the house for the big night. There wasn't a store in the village she hadn't visited buying food and odds and ends used for entertaining. It was to be the party of the year as she had invited most of the men and their wives from the place of Jim's employment. She bustled through the village shops for days carrying home parcel after parcel.

Finally the night arrived and the window in the house next door shone with candle light. Edna took her seat at the window to watch. Carriages arrived until the front yard was full. Everything seemed to be shaping up into a very happy evening. She sat back in her chair and tried to imagine what might be happening behind closed doors.

Suddenly the front doors opened and one after one couples returned to their carriages and pulled away. There was total silence. Not the excitement of people saying goodnight to friends after an enjoyable evening together. It seemed more like a mixed crowd, some friends some unknown to each other leaving church after a funeral of a mutual friend. Soon all were gone and the house became quiet. She sat for some time until finally the door opened once again and Jim emerged. He turned and made his way over the hill toward the village. She watched until he was out of sight and then turned her attention back to the house. Something had to be wrong and Bridgett would surely follow him to the village where all would be explained.

Leaning forward she strained to see into the house next door. Her window faced the dining room where she could see candles lit not only on the table but around the room as well. Standing at one end she could make out a figure she assumed must be Bridgett. She was standing very still with both hands over her eyes as though weeping. Edna wondered if she should go to her but thought better of it when she thought of her father's reaction. Then Bridgett moved to the table and stood for a moment then lifted her arm holding it above her head. One by one the candles went out until the room was completely dark and Edna could see no more.

Edna came to in a start and realized she had been thinking in the past. It had been some time since she had thought about the party and what had happened after that night. Both Bridgett and Jim had left the village according to her father and that was the end of it. Still there had been stories after and mostly about witchcraft. The house had been closed and no one lived there for many years.

She remembered a man and wife coming at one point but they had just looked things over and made arrangements for Joe to continue on as caretaker. They had also made financial arrangements for the house to be cared for then left never to return. It wasn't until many years later that a young woman, Karen came to claim the house as hers and stayed for a short time. Still she too left under mysterious circumstances and left the house to her cousin Rachel, the young woman who lived there now. This one had also purchased the empty store on Main Street that had once belonged to Rebecca, a cousin to Bridgett. Four cousins all bequeathed the house.

It seemed as though the house was coming full circle at last. Edna sighed deeply and sat back in her rocking chair by the window. One final peek told her that the two women she had been seeing were still looking down at her. Both raised their hands and waved. Edna squinted to see the faces more clearly and was finally able to recognize not just Bridgett but the face in the other window as well. A chill ran through her realizing that both women, Bridgett and Karen were finally back in the house.

— CHAPTER 48 —

Jessie closed the door to the shop. Dan had come again and stayed to tea and biscuits. She was sure that she hadn't encouraged him but he seemed to be showing a great deal of attention her way. Jessie had always been shy and had spent most of her free time alone or she would spend her off hours with Rebecca learning about the potions the older woman made after the store was closed each night.

She knew they were more than just face creams as the women of the village would not buy them during store hours but had them delivered to their homes when the men were out. When she questioned Rebecca about this the old woman told her she would learn when the time was right. Then Rebecca died and the right time had never come. Now she was left to ponder over the many books in the shop to find the answer for herself.

Reaching back she checked the lock on the door to be sure the shop was safe for the night and made her way back to the living quarters that now were hers. There was still one trunk that she had not opened and decided that it was early enough tonight to do this. Entering the small bedroom she went to the closet and pulled the somewhat battered little trunk into the centre of the room. Pulling the ring of keys from her pocket she inserted the smallest one into the rusty lock and turned it.

It took a bit of time for the lock to catch as the trunk had not been opened since before Rebecca died. Even some time before that probably for Jessie could not recall having seen it until she moved into the small living quarters. Her hand shook with excitement as the lock gave way and the trunk lid opened to the treasure beneath. Jessie gazed down into the contents with surprise for it was not recipes for the prized formulas but just a set of black dishes. It seemed like a complete set and Jessie started lifting them out one by one and setting them on the floor. When she finally pulled the last one from the bottom she found there was also a small black book. Now she thought this is probably what I was looking for. Leaning back against the trunk she opened the book and began to read.

— CHAPTER 49 —

Sheriff Hennessey was just leaving his office as Dan left the gift shop. He decided he would check with the sheriff to see if there was any news of Jack's whereabouts. It was a real concern to everyone who knew him. Like Josh he had never been known to leave the village even for a holiday. Also, he was a good family man with no problems to speak of, so it was a mystery when he disappeared.

Josh was beside himself and finally confided in Dan about the things he and Jack were looking into regarding the Warren house. It seemed that they were never going to be free of the stigma attached to it or the rest of the village. Since his talk with Josh about Jack's disappearance Dan had also spent a few hours at the library going through the village records. This with what the sheriff had turned up in the village records was beginning to take on a sinister tone.

He waved the sheriff down and headed in his direction. Both men turned up the street towards the coffee shop with the intention of comparing notes. Suddenly the sky turned fiery red and both men were overcome with the smell of heavy smoke.

Thinking it was a fire they began to run towards the area that the smoke seemed to be coming from.

Turning the corner they stopped dead in their tracks for there was no smoke and the sky once more returned to its normal dusk. With sudden shock they realized they were standing at the gate to the village square and the smell was of old smoke. Smoke from many fires long forgotten and tucked away in the history of the village.

It seemed now tucked away things had not been concealed as much as the village thought. Now one of their own had disappeared with undertones no one could answer. Jack had been too well liked in the village to simply write him off. Dan and Josh decided they would clear up this mystery as soon as they returned. For now however, the mystery of the smoke in the square would have to be looked into.

— CHAPTER 50 —

Rachel sat at the kitchen table with the book open before her. Her eyes were very tired from the length of time she had been reading. She found she just couldn't put the book down. She had no idea where she found it or how she ended up at the kitchen table but it was like she was compelled to read until it was finished. It was written like a diary by a young newlywed by the name of Bridgett who had come with her husband to live in the house.

She had been very happy at first but after a dinner party she gave for her husband's friends at work things seemed to take a turn. She remembered when she first came to the house how everything seemed so wonderful but now she felt alone and disoriented with no explanation. Like tonight Rachel seemed to be finding herself propelled into different parts of the house not knowing how she got there. There had also been the strong smell of roses in the staircase whenever she went into the front hall. In the book she had found reference to this at the time that Bridgett lived here.

She found the roses comforting and taking the book with her went into the hallway. Immediately the scent was upon her and she sat on the staircase to breathe it in. She felt at home here more than anywhere else in the house. Rachel thought of Jessie at the store and wondered if she could run things without her, as she would be more than content to just stay here forever.

Leaning her head against the wall she felt herself being lifted slowly up the staircase into the fragrance of the flowers. Suddenly there were voices whispering her name. Soft loving voices of young women calling her to come to them. They lulled her softly towards the wall where two pair of hands reached out and slowly pulled her gently out of sight.

CHAPTER 51

Jessie sat up with a start and rubbed her eyes. She found she was in the same place she had been for the last hour since Dan left. She couldn't help thinking there was something that he wanted from her and that it was right here in the store. She had gone over everything that belonged to Rebecca except for the small trunk in the closet. This was where she had found the book she had been reading for the past hour.

This is where she had found the story about Nora Preston, a respected teacher in the village. Children had loved Nora and she had been well liked by all who knew her. She was active in many of the women's groups in the community and with the local church helping at the bake sales and church jumble sales. It had been because of these that she had suddenly fallen from the ladies favour.

Two of the local women, Ada Simmons, wife of the local butcher and Mary Stewart, wife of the local barber were not as taken with Nora as the rest of the ladies. Their husbands were both business men and served on the general council. This they thought gave them a certain status over the other women and they used it whenever possible.

It was at one of the church sales that both women had bought food that Nora had prepared. All seemed well until both women became violently ill. Since there was no other reason that they could see and since they were not overly fond of Nora they accused her of trying to poison them. Others had also eaten the food with no ill effects and reasoned it had to be something else.But the women were not to be proven wrong and lose face so they rounded up their husbands and accused Nora of being a witch.

The men on their wives word went to Nora's home and taking her to the square without a trial had her burned at the stake. There had been many trials at this time with permanent spots set up in the town square to burn the people found guilty of being witches that day in court. Every night the fires burned and every morning the smoke still lingered over the village. Women stayed to their homes even afraid to attend their church on Sunday for fear of being accused by their friends and neighbours. After the night that Nora was burned the village took on a different tone. The trials were ended and the stakes were taken down. People skirted the town square with eyes lowered and handkerchiefs to their nose to cover the burning smell that still remained to this day.

Jessie woke with a start. She had slept the night on the floor of the shop. She pulled herself up with the book still in her hands. She looked down at the black dishes at her feet. Jessie knew now why she had been brought to Rebecca so many years ago. This was the reason Rebecca was teaching her. Rebecca was a witch. All the potions she had been selling the village women had been bewitched and were necessary to come to an end. Bridgett, Karen and now Rachel all belonged to the house and also poor Nora who had not been guilty, just disliked. She knew how that felt as most of her life she had been shunned by the people.

Picking up the dishes she packed them in a carton box and tied them closed. She would take them back to the house and complete what Rebecca started. It was time. She picked up the box of dishes and made her way to the front door. She fondly touched the counter and shelving on her way out and fingered each bit of china and paper. This had been her dream come true and now it was about to end. Locking the door behind her she stood for one final look at what had been her home for many years. From somewhere far off she heard the voice of Rebecca telling her what she must do. She stood for one moment longer then turning the key in the lock for the final time she made her way to the house and the women who owned it.

CHAPTER 52

Sheriff Hennesey decided it was time to change tactics. It had been a week now since Jack Simmons had disappeared. He had put all his men on double watch detail but no one had come up with a clue of any kind. It was as if Jack had stepped off the edge of the world into another dimension. Josh Stewart had been living in his back pocket since the day Jack disappeared and he wanted very much to be rid of him. To this end he had arranged for a meeting with Josh and himself this night to decide the best way to go from here.

As he was letting himself into the office he had met Dan Purcell and old Joe just leaving the café next door. Thinking there could be safety in numbers he asked them to join him. When they agreed he opened the door to the station and led them to his office. He found Josh there waiting for him so he settled back in his chair to review what they already knew.

Dan had very little to offer but Joe remembered when Jack's car had been found at the end of the Warren house road. He had passed it on his way to work that morning. He had stopped to look things over in case Jack was still with the car and needing assistance but the car was empty and nothing seemed disturbed. Continuing on he had pulled up his truck and unloaded the tools he would need for the day. He started with circling the house and checking all the gardens for anything that needed repair as he always did.

Reaching the back corner of the house he checked the outside entrance to the root cellar to be sure nothing was amiss as it was always left open in case he needed extra tools he stored there. He was surprised to find that the door had been locked from the inside. He decided that since it was a new owner, they were insecure in a new place. Thinking no more about it he went about his work for the day.

When he left at lunchtime the car was no longer there and he simply put it out of his mind. Now however he wondered if possibly Jack had gone into the cellar looking for him and locked himself in. Since the root cellar was made entirely of large boulders taken from the property a person could be shut in there for days with no one hearing their call for help.

Startled by the thought the sheriff pushed back his chair and grabbed his hat. The other three men rose also as it occurred to them that Jack may have been locked in that basement without food or water for a week and no way to escape. They rushed to their cars and tore up the road to the Warren house. Josh shuddered at the thought of his friend being closed in there for a week a prisoner of the Warren house. That was exactly the way he thought of it. A prisoner of the Warren house.

— CHAPTER 53 —

Jessie pulled up to a dark house. She was surprised thinking that Rachel would be home and she could just leave the box with her. This might have complicated things as she had a mission to perform for Rebecca and it was important that it be done at the right time. So it was better that Rachel was not home. No matter she had a way in. She reached into her pocket for the house keys that Rachel had given her and opened the front door.

A rush of rose fragrance brought her to her knees and the box she was holding slid across the floor. She heard the tinkle of glass as it came to a stop at the far wall. Oh please, she thought after all this time don't let anything happen to spoil things. The smell of roses began to fade and as it did her head began to clear. She sat for a moment longer until the air was fresh again then came to her feet.

Moving across the room she picked up the box of dishes and checked them for breaks. There were none. With a sigh of relief she made her way to the staircase. Part way up was a small landing and it was here that she placed the box of dishes.

She paused for a moment listening to the quiet of the house around her, then reaching out she hesitantly touched the soft rose petals on the wall. A soft voice told her she must go. She let the rose petal she was holding drop back into the pattern of the wallpaper and made her way to the front door. As she made her way up the hall she found her steps slowing and had to make an effort to even take a step. The walls seemed to be folding in around her.

She pushed forward, keeping to the centre of the hallway. She was afraid to touch the walls on either side as there seemed to be a pull she was afraid she would not be able break free of. With one final thrust she fell against the door and grasped the handle. Opening the door she stepped out onto the front stoop and without looking back closed the door for the last time behind her.

— CHAPTER 54 —

Sheriff Hennessey was about to turn down the lane to the Warren house when a car driven by Jessie pulled out. She waved cheerfully as she passed and continued into town. Well at least someone was home he thought. He would have no trouble checking out the basement. After a week he didn't want any further hold ups in finding Jack. He pulled in the turnaround and waited for the others to arrive.

While he waited he would just take a look around the house to see if there was a window open that might have let Jack out had he been in there. No the rest of the basement was sealed tight with no windows to the outside and only the one door to let you in or out. As he passed the side of the house he noticed the flutter of curtains at the house next door. Well he thought at least Edna was at her post and if there was something to worry about she would have called him. He was about to cross over into her yard when the rest of the men arrived. Keeping this thought in mind for later he went out front to join them.

The four men made their way to the front door and waited while the sheriff knocked several times with no answer. He was about to tell the men that they would have to come back when Josh suddenly pushed past him and began pounding on the door. Before the Sheriff could stop him the door flew open giving them entrance into the house. For just a moment the men stood frozen in their tracks. They had not expected this to happen and were not quite sure what to do.

Then without knowing why Dan moved ahead of everyone and stepped into the front hall. Everything was quiet. There was no breeze and the sun shone brightly across the polished floor. One by one the men stepped over the threshold and into the house. As the last man entered the house a strong smell of roses filled the air. Soon it was joined by the fragrance of lilacs and violets. As they stood in the centre hall they watched the sun slowly fade to be replaced by dark ominous shadows. Before anyone could move the heavy front door closed sealing them in forever.

No one had noticed as Jessie's car pulled over to the side of the road. She sat for a moment until the last car pulled up the lane to the Warren house. She had only to wait until all the men were in the house to finish her job. Slowly she turned her car around and headed back towards the house. She was just in time to see the front door close.

As she stepped from her car she noticed the curtains on the house next door open slightly. This too would be part of the plan she had to attend to. She reached into her bag and took out several pieces of rope and a book of matches. From the back seat she took gas cans and set them around the house. She then dropped one end of each rope into the cans. Looking up she saw Edna standing at her downstairs window. She laid gas cans under there as well. Bringing the other end of all the ropes together she poured gas on them until they were soaked.

Then striking a match she dropped it on the rope and hurried to her car.

Looking back all she could see were clouds of dark smoke and bright flames reaching for the sky. She glanced toward the house next door and saw Edna with her face pressed to the window. She saw her lift her hand just as the flames engulfed her. Jessie turned and without another backward glance stepped into her car and pulled up the lane. It was done. She smiled to herself as she caught the smell of roses and reaching over patted the two small books lying beside her on the seat. Then picking up speed she drove out on the road and away from the past.

— EPILOGUE —

In the end only the hill that divided the houses from the village remained. Peaceful silence settled over all as the last embers smouldered in the early morning light. At last the land was bare. Then from the last smoke of the houses came a whispered sound, take my hand, weaving its way up the hill.

Nora opened her eyes and gazed across the square. She was alone. Beneath her feet the grass once so green was now singed from the many fires recently lit there. Everything was quiet except for a voice reaching out to her. Take my hand. She slipped from the smouldering mound on which she had been standing and followed the sound.

The moon had long since left its place in the sky leaving everything pitch black. There was no movement. Then a vapour rose taking shape as it reached the top of the hill. She made her way gathering lilies as she went till she arrived at the top. One by one shapes appeared until there were four women standing hand in hand across the horizon. Then one by one they cast into the still rising smoke, a bunch of roses, a bunch of lilacs, a bunch of violets and finally a bunch of yellow lilies. A deep silence lay across the surrounding land. There were no birds or night sounds to be heard. It was as though no one had ever been here. No flower had ever grown and no rabbit had ever scurried through the bush away from pursuing hunters. It was as though death had taken over the entire area leaving nothing behind. To the right was the smouldering ruins of what had once been a magnificent country home. Now just a pile of burnt wood and broken bricks. Its neighbour who had for so long been the protector of this glorious mansion also lay in ruins at its feet. The smoke billowed into the trees taking heart and souls of both houses with it. What was left was just a solemn reminder of what they had been.

To the left of the houses the sky was lit as if a hundred torches were being carried by a crowd coming up the hillside. You could almost hear them chanting as they marched up the hill towards the stately mansion. It was a march repeated over the years that would be no more. On a closer look the light of the torches became flames weaving their way through the trees. Soon there would be nothing left but barren ground that once had been a quaint little village close to the sea. All was engulfed in flame. There was no sound of barking dogs or the cries of children. Nor was there the sound of men shouting as they hurried to distinguish the flames. Only the hungry sound of the fire as it gulped and swallowed the shop and houses that had once been Blakesville.

www.ingramcontent.com/pod-product-compliance
Lightning Source LLC
LaVergne TN
LVHW091555060526
838200LV00036B/842